What On Earth Was I Thinking? Susannah Asked Herself. How Could I Have Given Myself To This Man?

She swallowed hard. The sun glinted off Amado's proud profile. His sleeves were rolled up to reveal tanned and muscled forearms. He was gorgeous.

But that was no excuse. She'd have to do her best to stay far away from him while he was in New York. Then he'd go back to Argentina, and no one would be any the wiser.

"Why are you backing away from me?"

She froze, unaware that her body had been trying to put a safe distance between them. "I'm not."

"Yes, you are." He took a step toward her. Desire throbbed in her veins as her body responded to the raw power of his gesture. "But don't think you can walk away from me now...."

Dear Reader,

The seed for this book was planted while I was out walking with my friend and neighbor, Ana, and she mentioned that her family came from Argentina's wine country. Once I learned that the Mendoza wine-growing region is nestled at the foot of the majestic Andes mountains and irrigated by melt water from the snowy peaks, I became fascinated.

In recent years the area has experienced a boom in productivity and popularity, since local altitudes and sun exposure combine to create a *terroir* that produces unique and intense flavors. I learned a lot about the passionate wine makers of the area and their beautiful estates from www.vinesofmendoza.com and naturally I also enjoyed some delicious liquid research.

This land of colorful history, breathtaking scenery and rich flavors seemed the perfect setting for a tale of intrigue and passion. I hope you enjoy Susannah and Amado's story.

Jennifer Lewis

JENNIFER LEWIS

IN THE ARGENTINE'S BED

Published by Silhouette Books
America's Publisher of Contemporary Romance

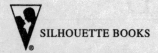

SILHOUETTE BOOKS

ISBN-13: 978-0-373-76931-5
ISBN-10:   0-373-76931-8

Recycling programs
for this product may
not exist in your area.

IN THE ARGENTINE'S BED

Visit Silhouette Books at www.eHarlequin.com

Printed in U.S.A.

Books by Jennifer Lewis

Silhouette Desire

The Boss's Demand #1812
Seduced for the Inheritance #1830
Black Sheep Billionaire #1847
Prince of Midtown #1891
Millionaire's Secret Seduction #1925
In the Argentine's Bed #1931

*The Hardcastle Progeny

JENNIFER LEWIS

has been dreaming up stories for as long as she can remember and is thrilled to be able to share them with readers. She has lived on both sides of the Atlantic and worked in media and the arts before she grew bold enough to put pen to paper. Happily settled in New York with her family, she would love to hear from readers at jen@jen-lewis.com. Visit her Web site at www.jenlewis.com.

To Ana, my ally in many adventures.

Acknowledgment:

Thanks once again to the generous people who read
this book while I was writing it, including Amanda,
Anne, Betty, Carol, Cynthia and Leeanne, and my agent
Andrea. Special thanks to Liliana and Marina, creators
of www.universeofromance.com.ar/harlequineras
for their enthusiasm and assistance.

One

How do you make a complete stranger hand over his DNA?

Susannah Clarke's rental car was almost totally out of gas. She'd known the Tierra de Oro *estancia* was well outside Mendoza, Argentina, and had planned accordingly. But the car and its fuel tank were tiny, and everything else here was on a much grander scale than she'd imagined.

Including her own trepidation.

To her right, the sun glittered amongst the high, snow-dusted peaks of the Andes. Around her lay the fertile plain that supported some of the finest vineyards in the world.

As she turned off the highway, the needle on the fuel meter hovered below zero. Come on, just a little farther. She didn't want to run out of gas and have to walk the rest of the way to the house with her news. "Hey, I think you're my boss's illegitimate son—got a gallon of gas to spare?"

She swallowed hard as a building came into view.

Deep breath.

She eased off the accelerator, anxious to stretch the last few drops of gas as far as they'd go. Rows of cypress trees now lined the drive, shading it from the bright sun. An elegant painted sign pointed to the right, where she could see a large brick structure against the backdrop of mountains. The Tierra de Oro *Bodega,* or winery.

She pressed on toward the house. For once she wasn't coming to talk to the chief viticulturist about which kinds of grapes thrived in the local soils or how many cases Hardcastle Enterprises wanted for its flagship restaurant.

The avenue of cypress widened into a lush garden, surrounding a lovely old house with a red-tiled roof and wide, arched windows.

This is it.

She pulled the stick-shift car to a jerky stop in front of the paneled wood doorway. She opened the car door and stepped out, her heart thudding.

Then she heard the barking. Loud, guttural and getting closer with every second. Two huge white dogs bounded around the side of the house and careened toward her across the gravel.

Holy—

Susannah staggered back and struggled with the car door handle, her brain crowded with visions of being eaten alive on Amado Alvarez's doorstep.

It wouldn't open.

The worn door handle had apparently done enough work today.

"Help!" she finally cried, in Spanish, as the first giant animal leaped toward her, jaws wide.

It jumped on her, knocking her against the car as the other dog barked and growled from a few feet away. Pain shot through her elbow when it collided with the half-open window. "Help!"

The front door flew open and she heard a gruff male command. The dogs immediately backed away and sat, panting innocently. Susannah struggled to catch her breath, still flattened against the side of her tiny rental car.

A tall man came down the steps in a loping stride. "I apologize for my dogs' overenthusiastic greeting."

He spoke in Spanish. And why wouldn't he? He had no idea who she was.

His dark brown hair dipped seductively to almond-shaped eyes. The soft drape of his khakis and cream-colored shirt revealed broad shoulders, slim hips and long, powerful legs.

He was handsome.

And about thirty. The age of Tarrant Hardcastle's missing son.

Her heart, already pumping hard from the near-death encounter, beat faster.

She shoved out her hand. "At least you don't have to worry about burglars."

He smiled. A slightly lopsided grin. White teeth against suntanned skin. Susannah found her heart fluttering for reasons that had nothing to do with fear as he grasped her palm in a warm handshake.

Did she imagine it, or did he give her hand a suggestive squeeze? Mischief shimmered in those wicked brown eyes.

Susannah was good at reading people and she could tell this man was used to getting his way.

His features were aristocratic, elegant. His long, slightly aquiline nose tapering to tear-shaped nostrils. Everything about him telegraphed ease and comfort in his surroundings.

He snapped his fingers and the two giant hounds scampered to his feet and crouched there, tongues hanging, as they gazed adoringly up at him. "Apologize to the lady." He raised his hand in a gesture, and the dogs immediately turned. Then he snapped his fingers and they sprawled at her feet.

"I'm impressed."

"Cástor and Pólux are usually well-behaved. I don't know why they got so worked up." He paused, and let his arrogant gaze drift over the front of her blue jacket to the loose flowered cotton of her skirt. "Then again, maybe I do." His eyes glittered with suggestion. "How may I help you?"

"Are you Amado Alvarez?"

"At your service." He lowered his head in a mock bow. "Your name?"

"Susannah Clarke." Susannah took a deep breath. "I…I have a private matter to discuss with you."

His elegant brow crinkled slightly. "How intriguing. Do come in." He indicated the wide stone steps in front of the open door.

He stood to one side as she climbed past him, her elbow still smarting from where his dog had smashed her against the car.

Of course, the news she brought might leave Amado Alvarez with far more than a bruised elbow.

He ushered her into a large living room with comfortable sofas arranged around a grand fireplace. The patter of massive dog feet followed them over the tiled floors.

"A private matter, you say?" He indicated for her to sit on one of the leather sofas. He sat next to her, but with enough distance to be polite. The dogs sprawled on a patterned rug in front of the unlit fireplace.

"Yes." She knitted her fingers together. "Have you ever heard of Tarrant Hardcastle?"

Blood pounded in Susannah's brain as he contemplated the question.

He shrugged. "No, should I have?"

"Well—" She twisted her fingers. If she blew this she could lose her job. "I'm not really sure how to say this, but he believes he's your father and he'd like very much to meet with you."

Amado's eyes narrowed and his mouth widened into that crooked smile. "Is this some kind of joke? Who put you up to this? Tomás?"

She inhaled. "I'm afraid it's not a joke. Tarrant believes he had an affair with your mother in Manhattan, back in the late 1970s, and that you are the result of that union."

Amado's face creased with amusement. "Manhattan? In New York?"

"Yes. She was there studying art. At least, that's how Tarrant remembers it."

Amado looked at her as if she'd just sprouted a third eye. "My mother…was studying art in New York City?" He let out a guffaw.

He turned his head. "Mamá!" His voice rang across the room. Susannah cringed as he called for his mother. A woman probably now in her fifties and living a respectable life, about to be confronted with a single indiscretion from many years ago that could upturn all of their lives.

She shrank into the sofa.

"What is it, sweetheart?" called a soft voice. Susannah rose to her feet as his mother entered the room. A short, rotund woman with fluffy gray hair, thick-framed glasses and navy orthopedic shoes.

Susannah blinked. Mrs. Alvarez was a stark contrast to Tarrant's ex-beauty-queen, third wife.

Amado rose and kissed her. "Mamá, you're going to

love this. First, let me introduce you. Susannah Clarke, this is my mother, Clara Alvarez."

"Delighted to meet you." Clara shook Susannah's hand gently. Her skin was soft, like her voice. Her pale blue eyes sparkled with warmth. "Have you traveled far?"

Susannah swallowed hard. "From New York."

"Mamá, have you ever been to New York?"

Susannah could swear the older woman—and she looked to be close to seventy—suddenly changed. Her bearing stiffened, and her expression hardened. "Never."

"Susannah seems to think you were studying art there in the 1970s."

Clara Alvarez laughed. Not a natural laugh, though. A sharp, forced one. "What nonsense. I've never been farther than Buenos Aires. Why would she think such a crazy thing?"

Her eyes gleamed with suspicion—and reproof—as she glared at Susannah over the rims of her glasses.

Susannah hesitated. It was impossible to imagine Tarrant having an affair with this…little old lady. Even thirty years ago, she'd have been middle-aged. Tarrant's current wife was half his age, if that.

"Excuse me, I have a pot on the stove." Clara excused herself and bustled away.

"See what I mean?" Amado raised an eyebrow. "It pains me to say this, but I think you have the wrong Amado Alvarez."

Susannah frowned. Alvarez was a common name…. Could the researcher have made a mistake?

Tierra de Oro was the right place, though. And she'd been ordered not to return to Hardcastle Enterprises without a sample of *this* Amado Alvarez's DNA.

Time was of the essence. Tarrant Hardcastle had already

outlived his doctor's projections, and if he was to meet his missing son before it was too late…

"The matter could be cleared up with a simple test. If you'd be so kind as to give me a DNA sample, I could get it processed immediately and we'd know the truth one way or the other."

Amado's eyes widened. "DNA? You want my blood?"

"It doesn't have to be blood. In fact, a scraping from inside your mouth would be ideal."

He clapped a large hand against one side of his face as if someone might attempt to gouge into it. "No."

Clara reappeared, tugging a silver-haired man who stared at Susannah. Clara whispered so rapidly that Susannah couldn't make out the words.

The dogs rose to their feet, sniffing tension in the air.

The older man strode up to Susannah and nodded a brusque greeting. "Young lady, I am Ignacio Alvarez and Amado is my son. Your business here is concluded. Allow me to escort you to your car."

This man had brown eyes, like Amado, whereas Tarrant had blue. If Tarrant and Clara had an affair, surely Amado would have blue eyes?

"I…I," Susannah groped for the right thing to say. If she went home without the DNA, Tarrant would be furious.

He'd probably fire her.

Or send her right back here.

Or both.

"Papá, I'm shocked at you." Amado frowned and stepped between his father and Susannah. "This young woman may be mistaken in her quest, but she's traveled all the way from New York and we've not even offered her refreshments."

Susannah glanced from one man to the other. Amado

was tall, over six foot—like Tarrant—whereas Ignacio was probably only five-eight or so. Still…

"Son, I really think that—"

Amado held up his hand. "Allow me to offer you a snack and some coffee. Or would you prefer wine?"

Susannah drew in a breath. "I'm a wine buyer for Hardcastle Enterprises." Perhaps she could try to turn this into a business trip and come back to the more personal part later. "I'd love to sample your wines with a view to purchasing them for our restaurants."

"Excellent. Mamá, please ask Rosa to prepare a bite for our guest. And a glass of the 2004 Malbec, to start."

Susannah turned to find Ignacio staring at her, brows lowered. She jerked her gaze away. No surprise he was upset that she'd suggested his son wasn't his.

Clara had vanished, possibly to slip poison into a glass of 2004 Malbec.

"Which varietals do you grow here at Tierra de Oro?" She put on a brave professional smile.

"Mostly Cabernet Sauvignon and Malbec, but we're fortunate to have a variety of elevations and microclimates, so we experiment constantly with new vines." Amado's expression had smoothed. He looked comfortable again. "Why don't we go outside and I'll show you?"

He led her across the living room, past the glaring Ignacio, and out onto a stone patio with a view over the southern portion of the estate. Row upon row of leafy vines traced the gentle contours of the land, rising into the foothills of the majestic Andes. The lush growth gave no hint of the effort needed to tease productive plants from the relatively arid soil of the area.

"It's a special place."

The words drifted out of Susannah's mouth without her

really meaning to say them. The light had a strange quality that rather dazzled her. Bright but somehow soft.

Harsh, yet…loving.

Maybe all those hours of travel had addled her brain.

Amado stared across the rolling terrain. "Yes. It is a special place." A frown gathered on his proud brow. "I can't imagine living anywhere else."

Susannah froze. It occurred to her that if Amado was not Ignacio's son, he might lose his right to run the estate.

Suddenly the afternoon sunlight seemed blinding.

"How long has your family been here?"

"Forever." He smiled. "Well, that's how it feels. The first Alvarez came here in 1868 from Cádiz and married a local girl. We've been here ever since."

"I can see why. It's beautiful."

The sun glinted off the snowcapped mountains. Vast and solid, they stretched almost to the end of the earth.

Susannah had never lived in one place for more than three years. She couldn't even blame her missionary parents anymore. She'd moved about on her own as an adult.

"It's changed a lot since then, of course, but we do our best to protect and care for the land."

"Have you always grown grapes here?" She was careful to imply he was part of the Alvarez family.

"There've always been a few hundred vines, mostly for family consumption. Most of these—" he swept his arm across the acres and acres of rows "—have been planted in the last ten to fifteen years since I convinced my father to switch from beef to viniculture."

The door behind them opened and a tiny, ancient woman, who made Clara look positively youthful by comparison, emerged carrying a tray with two glasses of wine and a plate with some pastries.

"Thank you, Rosa." Amado took the tray and placed it on the stone wall that ringed the patio. Susannah smiled at Rosa—who returned her gesture with a flinty stare.

Gulp.

"The 2004 Malbec is one of our bestsellers. It's won several awards and brought us international attention. See what you think." He held out the glass. His dark eyes shone with anticipation that revealed his pride in his wine.

Susannah took it and admired the dark ruby color of the liquid against the white peaks and pale blue of the sky. She sniffed the bouquet—young, fruity—perhaps too much so for her taste. Then she sipped. A tiny taste, just enough to test the mouth-feel and waken her taste buds to the experience.

Amado hovered over her in silent expectation.

"Delicious." No lie. It was bold and wonderful.

His lopsided grin revealed those even, white teeth as he raised his glass and sipped. "I agree. It's okay to be proud of one's own child, don't you think?"

"Absolutely." She couldn't help smiling. And sipping again. Enjoying the rich warm flavor of the sunbaked soil and the well-irrigated grapes grown in this stunning landscape. "How many cases do you have available for purchase?"

He threw back his head and laughed, giving her a lingering vision of his bronzed neck, muscles flexed, under the creamy-white collar of his shirt. "Getting down to business so soon? I've heard that you Americans don't like to waste time. They weren't kidding."

Susannah blinked. Was her professional interest in the wine somehow inappropriate under the circumstances?

She was sure Tarrant would want this for Moon, the five-star restaurant atop his Manhattan retail palace. It would be excellent with the chef's famous osso buco, and with the boeuf en croute. "Are you not interested in selling?"

"Of course I'm interested. Selling wine is my business." His expression suggested he found the whole subject vastly amusing.

"Then, why are you laughing at me?" She hated how defensive she sounded.

"You're so serious." He lifted the plate. "Try some of Rosa's *alfajores*."

She picked up one of the pastries. It was somewhere between a cookie and a sandwich. Two layers of pastry glued together with...

She bit in. Caramel. Or, more accurately, *dulce de leche. Yum.*

She flicked her tongue out to catch stray crumbs of pastry.

Amado's dark gaze rested on her mouth. "Rosa is the finest cook in all of Mendoza."

"I won't argue with you. How many cases of these can I buy?"

He laughed, and she was relieved that at least now she had him laughing with her and not at her. But it was time to get back to her real business here. "Your parents seemed upset."

He frowned. "Yes."

Susannah took a deep breath. "As if they know something." She hesitated, waiting for him to draw his own conclusions.

He looked out at the bright mountain peaks silhouetted against the clear blue sky. And didn't say a word.

"They wanted to get rid of me because they don't want you to hear what I have to say." She stared right at him. "You know that, don't you?"

He blinked. "I agree that their behavior was odd."

Susannah sensed that confusion was a rare and difficult

emotion for Amado Alvarez. He didn't know quite how to deal with it. He wanted to say *No, you're wrong*.

But he couldn't.

Amado watched the summer breeze play in her long, dark hair and pull at the loose skirt of her dress. Slender and nervous, the lovely Susannah seemed embarrassed by her invasion of his privacy.

As well she might be.

What kind of mad story was this? Of course, he should dismiss it out of hand. He had in his office a birth certificate naming Clara and Ignacio as his parents. Ignacio had made a point of presenting it to him and telling him to keep it safe.

But why had his mother and father reacted so strangely to her arrival? They'd had some obnoxious visitors in the past, folks who'd enjoyed the wine too much, but he'd never seen his parents be less than civil.

What was going on?

He stepped closer, until he could smell her scent. Subtle, floral, in keeping with her demure, businesslike persona. "Why did you come here on this strange errand?"

"Tarrant Hardcastle is my boss. I travel for the company sourcing wines. I'm pretty sure I was chosen because I'm fluent in seven languages, including Spanish. Tarrant's daughter Fiona offered to come, but they weren't sure you'd speak English."

"I do, you know," he replied, in English.

"So I see." She smiled, which revealed a row of delicate teeth. "Then they needn't have sent me at all, but here I am." She shrugged. "I do love my job and I'd like to keep it."

"And for that you require a few ounces of my life's blood." He had no intention of complying with her request, but she was so serious that he couldn't resist the urge to tease her.

"As I said before, a swab from the inside of your mouth…"

Amado winced, then an entertaining idea occurred to him. "Could you perhaps obtain it with a kiss?"

Her eyes widened, and he saw a flush of color deepen the smooth skin of her cheeks. Lovely.

She regained control of herself and lifted an eyebrow. "You mean take a cheek cell culture with my tongue?"

The thought of that quick pink tongue in his mouth made a predatory smile creep across his lips. "That, I might be able to subject myself to. If you were willing, of course."

"I don't think that would be very scientific. My DNA would be mixed in with yours."

"All the better." He stared at her mouth until her lips parted.

"Ha ha ha." Her laugh sounded tinny and false. Good. He was making her nervous.

He cocked his head. "I'm ready and willing. You can take your sample right now, if you like."

She narrowed her lovely dark eyes. "My best friend warned me about Argentine men."

"Oh?" He let his gaze drift over her face and neck. Enjoyed the sensual curve of her mouth and the proud tilt of her chin.

She put her hands on her hips. "She said they're very arrogant. Full of themselves."

He fought the urge to say *Yeah, and?*

But he didn't resist letting his eyes wander lower, to where her stance pulled her jacket taut over her firm, high breasts, then down to where her propped hands defined her waist all too sharply.

Her hips twitched slightly under his gaze. Desire crept through him. He couldn't help staring as a sudden breeze pressed her gauzy skirt to her long, slim legs.

Susannah took her hands off her hips and crossed her arms defensively over her chest.

"I've never had a beautiful woman ask for my DNA before. I'm just considering all my options." Amado raised his eyes again and confronted her with his open admiration.

Her prim and proper demeanor triggered an urge to see her unbuttoned and breathless. He'd like to take her to his bed and pleasure her. Make her forget all about DNA and someone's child and the whole crazy idea.

"Why does your boss think that I, out of all the people in the world, am his son?"

"He hired a researcher a few months ago. I think he told her all he knew about the mothers, and when they'd had the children."

Revulsion rose in his gut. "This man thinks he has several children he's never met?"

She nodded. "It's awkward. I haven't met the researcher, but I was told they'd located you here. Maybe they're just fishing in the hope that you're the right person."

"I can't be, you know." It simply wasn't possible.

She shrugged and a half smile tilted her mouth. Tickled his urge to kiss it. "It does seem unlikely. I'm only here because I was asked to come."

"Do you always do what you're told?" He raised a brow.

"It depends on who's asking, and how much I trust them."

Her honest answer only intrigued him more.

"Then how about I'll give you a sample of my DNA—just to prove you're wrong, of course—if you'll spend the night in my bed."

Two

Susannah's mouth hung open for a second before she managed a laugh. "That's one way to collect DNA. I'm not sure your parents would approve."

Ignacio Alvarez burst through the doors onto the patio as if he'd been listening. Susannah recoiled in horror at the realization that he probably had. Clara followed close behind him, plucking anxiously at his jacket.

Cool and calm, Amado raised the bottle. "Will you join us for some wine?"

Ignacio's bushy silver brows lowered. "Amado, we have urgent business to discuss."

"I can imagine no business more urgent than entertaining Miss Clarke. As you heard, she's a buyer for an important New York wine retailer. We've spoken about bringing our wines to the States. This could be the opportunity we've been waiting for."

He shot her a sly wink.

Susannah managed to keep her features composed.

"She's arrived unannounced. There is no record of her appointment." Ignacio glared at her.

Tarrant's office had made multiple calls trying to set up an appointment, and had been pointedly ignored. Most likely by Ignacio. That was the reason she'd been forced to arrive unannounced.

Her curiosity deepened. She glanced at Clara, who stood in the doorway, eyes wide and anxious.

"Dad, why does Susannah's presence here make you so uncomfortable? Surely you don't believe her crazy story about me being her boss's illegitimate son?" He smiled as if it was a great joke.

Ignacio's weathered brow creased into a frown. "Of course not," he growled. "It's ridiculous and downright offensive. I don't wish base accusations to tarnish our reputation. Who knows what ugly rumors such scandalous talk might generate?"

"You can't have a rumor without something to talk about. And there's nothing to discuss, right?" Amado leveled a dark and challenging stare at his father. Clearly, his parents' odd behavior was making him suspicious.

And curious.

"She must leave, dear," Clara piped up in her soft voice. "It's for the best. We don't want people to talk." She wrung her plump hands.

"Have you both taken leave of your senses? Of course we want people to talk. We want the words 'Tierra de Oro' on everyone's lips." He tilted his chin to them, defying them to disagree. "I want Susannah to return to New York, unable to stop talking about our wines." He shot her a winning smile. "In fact, we were about to head to the winery, so I can make her comfortable in the tasting room."

Susannah's eyes widened. Still, she wasn't going to argue. As long as he wasn't throwing her out.

Ignacio spluttered and Clara issued a breathy plea for him to talk to his father, but Amado slipped his arm into Susannah's and led her past the troubled pair, through the living room, and out into the drive.

For a split second it occurred to her that he was going to pack her into her car. Get rid of her as his parents had demanded.

But instead he pulled open the passenger door of a large Mercedes sedan parked in the shade.

She climbed in, wondering if she'd live to regret it.

And if he'd live to regret not throwing her off the property. "You must be very close to your parents, to still live with them."

"They don't live here. They built a modern house near the winery. They're always hovering around, though. I think they worry about me. They keep badgering me to find a nice girl and settle down."

His wicked smile confirmed that he had no intention of obeying their wishes.

"They're right to be worried." Susannah raised an eyebrow. "You seem to be looking for trouble."

"You're wrong. Trouble has come looking for me."

His heavy lidded stare made her legs wobble.

She was in trouble. At least she would be if she didn't find a nice way to turn down his bold invitation to spend the night in his bed, yet still get her sample.

She couldn't go home without the sample. If it proved Amado wasn't Tarrant's son, then there might still be time to find the right person before Tarrant died. She couldn't forgive herself if incompetence on her part denied him the chance to meet his child. She had to get Amado to agree.

Still, she didn't want to press her point too hard and scare him off. He did seem intrigued by the prospect of doing business with Hardcastle Enterprises. Maybe she could somehow use that to persuade him to go along with her request.

She leaned back in the leather passenger seat and cleared her throat. "How many cases of wine do you produce each year?"

Amado chuckled, staring ahead out the windshield. "Changing the subject? I guess you don't need my DNA so badly after all." His lips hitched into a sensual smile. "I'm disappointed."

His gaze lingered. Would he dignify her question with an answer? And what would she do if he didn't?

She wished she could be a witty flirt like her best friend Suki. Being the daughter of devout missionaries didn't really prepare you for situations like this.

His big hands rested on the steering wheel. "Last year we produced nearly four thousand cases. This year, there'll be more, as several hundred new rows are coming into full production."

"You're growing fast."

"We have to if we're going to make a name for ourselves."

She nodded. "Are you trying to expand your markets overseas?"

"Absolutely. I'd especially like to expand into North America." His expression was entirely genuine, nothing sexual about it.

Somehow that touched her. "If your other wines are as good as this, I don't think you'll have any trouble securing distribution."

"We're still small, so it must be the right distribution. Outlets where our wines will reach the right people."

"Where they'll be appreciated."

"Exactly."

Amado drove the familiar road apparently by instinct. His eyes seemed mostly to rest on her face, which heated under his intense gaze.

She struggled to keep her composure. "I think Hardcastle Enterprises could do a lot for you. In addition to our restaurants, we offer a boutique wine-selecting service for our customers. We keep their cellars stocked with the very best wines available that year."

Amado's keen interest was written all over his handsome features as they pulled into a parking area behind the large, stone winery building. "I look forward to showing you our winery. I'm confident you'll enjoy our wines."

Susannah resisted a triumphant smile. Finally, she had some real leverage. If she played her cards right, she could get the DNA she needed.

Was it the flattering glow of sunset, or was Amado getting more ridiculously handsome than ever?

Susannah sat at a wide, polished table, rows of fine-stemmed glasses in front of her, their shimmering contents ranging in color from darkest garnet to palest silver.

Across the table, standing, Amado inhaled the bouquet of a youngish red, sipped it, then tossed his head back to swallow with a lavish gesture.

He'd rolled up his creamy-white sleeve to reveal a tan forearm, and she couldn't help imagining the rest of his body would be equally hard and well-formed.

The tasting room was warm, and she'd removed her jacket. Her nipples stood to attention inside the loose-fitting top of her dress. The curved chair with its velvet padding was deliciously comfortable after the long drive crunched into her tiny rental car, and she longed to stretch like a cat.

She felt downright…tipsy. She'd blame the wine, but as an experienced taster she knew how to sip tiny amounts that couldn't possibly get her inebriated.

At least she thought she did.

Amado poured Chardonnay into a glass. The pale liquid sparkled in the afternoon sun streaming in through the tall windows.

She inhaled then tasted. Flavor tingled across her tongue and caressed her throat with its smooth, golden warmth.

Like Amado, the wines seemed to be getting more delicious by the minute.

"Tierra de Oro—is there real gold in the earth around here?" She set the glass back on the table.

"I don't think so. If there ever was, it's long gone. The only gold around at Tierra de Oro is the kind stored in bottles." He caressed a stemmed glass of pale liquid between finger and thumb.

Susannah's belly shivered in response.

"I enjoy this kind of gold much more than the metal."

"It costs less per ounce but gives more pleasure." Amado's smile revealed his white teeth.

Why did he have to be so great-looking?

And she was entranced by the way he treated the wine like a sacred liquid. He handled the bottles as if they were sentient—firm yet gentle.

The way he might handle her if he removed her dress and layered kisses over her breasts and belly.

Susannah sat upright as a rush of heat swept through her. "It's getting late. I'd better go to my hotel."

Amado frowned. "What hotel?"

"Any hotel." She hadn't booked a room, as she wasn't sure if she'd have to stay locally, or if she could just head back to the city.

Apparently, she'd have to stick around for one more night to talk him into giving the DNA sample. What if he balked tomorrow, as well?

"There are no hotels here."

She groaned. The vineyard was over two hours from Mendoza. If she returned there for the night, she'd have to drive back here in the morning to resume her campaign.

"Where do people usually stay?"

He blinked. Innocent. "Here."

"At the winery?"

"In my house." He picked up a three-year-old Cabernet. The tapered glass bottle looked slender and delicate in his big hands.

She could picture those broad palms and long fingers spanning the dip of her waist. "I'd prefer a hotel."

He shrugged. "As I said. There isn't one. This is the country, not a tourist destination."

His polite smile warred with the mischievous gleam in his dark eyes. "And Rosa will cook you a very fine dinner."

"But what about your parents? They can't wait for me to leave."

"Don't worry about them. They have their own house and I've made my feelings clear. They won't interfere again." His expression softened. "You'll find my home quite comfortable. You're the only one here, so you can have your pick of the rooms. In the morning, we can conclude our business."

Perhaps he'd give her what she wanted if she stayed overnight. And it wasn't like she had anywhere else to go.

"It looks like I'm at your mercy. I mean, thanks for your hospitality."

He laughed. She couldn't help smiling. Truth be told, she didn't mind staying. Not because she had any intention of personally extracting Amado's DNA, but because everything about Tierra de Oro was so enchanting. The breathtaking views, the lush vines, the comfortable well-kept buildings.

And the wine had mellowed her out something wicked. She wasn't even sure she *should* drive. Not to mention that she still had no gas.

And she couldn't leave without his DNA.

"My offer still stands."

"Which offer was that?"

He leveled a challenging gaze at her. "Whichever one you prefer."

Susannah stowed her bag in a guest bedroom, committing herself to stay the night, one way or another.

As promised, dinner was sensational. A classic Argentine meal with locally raised steaks, fresh-picked vegetables and glass after glass of Amado's magnificent wines.

Silent and catlike, Rosa served their food in the grand dining room. Instead of family portraits, the walls were lined with oil paintings of massive, rectangular-shaped bulls, each frame adorned with a gold nameplate.

"I guess someone loved cows."

"My great grandfather. My grandfather. And my father." Amado sipped his wine. "Tierra de Oro was known throughout Argentina for its breeding stock."

"Do you still breed them?"

"My father does, but it's a hobby at this point. Not profitable. That's why I started the vineyard."

"You?"

"Yes." He looked at her quizzically. "Why are you surprised?"

"Well, you're only thirty." She blanched when she realized she'd assumed that the research was correct and he was in fact Tarrant's son. "Aren't you?"

"As it happens, I am thirty. But I was fooling around in the fields and growing things by the time I was eight. By age eleven, I'd hybridized a Syrah that got people talking. My neighbor Santos taught me a lot. He's ninety now and one of the true geniuses of winemaking. He helped me persuade my father to let me plant grapes in our pastures. By the time I was eighteen, we'd planted seventy hectares of vines." He nodded at her glass. "You're drinking their fruit now."

"So, you skipped right over watching *Power Rangers* and *Real World* TV shows."

Amado smiled. "When the TV broke, no one cared—except Rosa. She missed her telenovelas."

"Thank God your father finally came to his senses and bought a satellite dish." The silvery voice made Susannah whip her head around. Rosa stood right behind her. A stern expression still tightened her inscrutable and impossibly ancient face.

Amado laughed. "Now she's addicted to CNN broadcasts."

She clucked her tongue.

"Someone's got to keep the Alvarez family in touch with the modern world. Otherwise, all you'd do is fondle grapes and stick your hands up a cow's backside."

Susannah almost spewed her wine and Amado bent his head in laughter.

Rosa bustled away with an empty serving dish. Susannah leaned forward and whispered. "She's a character. How old is she?"

Amado blew out a breath. "Probably older than the mountains. She's certainly been here longer than anyone else. Every other person around here is her grandchild or great grandchild. For years I've been trying to convince her to retire and take it easy in her old age. She flaps her dishcloth at me and says she'd just as soon be dead."

"What do you *do* around here for fun?"

"What could be more fun than testing the soil for nitrates?" Amado tilted his head and regarded her with mock seriousness. "What can I say? I love my work."

"I know how you feel. I love mine, too." She indicated the delicious meal spread before them. "I'm working right now. It's a tough job, but, well, you know."

"You traveled a long way. The least I can do is give you a good meal."

"Much appreciated. I'm used to traveling though. I'm on the road about eighty percent of the time."

Amado's lips parted in dismay. "You're away from home most of the year?"

Susannah shrugged. "My home is a featureless, one-room apartment in a busy part of Manhattan. It's just a place to keep my stuff. I'm happiest when I'm out and about."

He stared at her. "Where are you from originally? I mean, where did you grow up?"

She forced a bright smile. *Here we go.* "Everywhere. I was born in a tiny village in the Philippines where my parents set up a primary school. When I was eighteen months old, my parents moved to Burkina Faso to take over a mission there. When I was three, we moved to Papua, New Guinea. I turned six in a small village in

Southern India, but that placement didn't work out, so I had my seventh birthday in Columbus, Ohio while my parents attended a retreat there. Then we were back on the road to Honduras, El Salvador, Paraguay and Bolivia, which is why I speak fluent Spanish."

The canned account of her strange childhood rattled out like a recorded recap.

"Your parents were missionaries?"

"You got it." She raised her glass in a mock cheer. She was used to the sideways glances and snide remarks. Her parents were good people and they did what they thought was right.

Surprise trickled through her as she noticed Amado wasn't mocking. He looked interested. "It must have been hard when you were a kid. To keep leaving your friends and your familiar environment."

She shrugged. "I never lived any other way, so I guess I'm used to it. Their specialty is setting up programs and finding the right local people to run them. Then they move onto the next place. I guess the lifestyle shaped me, because I'm happiest when I'm moving from place to place."

She realized Amado was staring at her with a look of…was it pity?

"What?"

He shook his head, as if shaking loose a painful thought. "Nothing. I guess it's great that you love to travel. Everyone's different."

"You're horrified, aren't you?"

"No." He laughed. "Okay, maybe a little. I don't even like to go away on business for a few days. I feel like my roots have been pulled from the soil and I can't wait to get back home and plant them among the grape vines again."

His wry expression suggested that he was a little embarrassed by his deep attachment to his home.

That touched her. What would it feel like to be so deeply rooted in a place—in one special place—that you felt like you truly belonged there?

Amado's brows gathered. "Are you okay? More wine?"

Her face must be giving too much away. "I guess I'm just tired from all the traveling."

He nodded, sympathetic. "Of course. Well, tonight, you are home in Tierra de Oro where I will take good care of you." He rose and held out his hand to lift her from her chair.

His genial gaze rested on her face. "Come into the living room and we'll light a fire. The nights are still cool and a fire warms the soul as well as the body."

Susannah blinked as his words and the touch of his hand stoked a very different kind of fire.

He held her hand—casually—as he led her into the spacious living room and settled her into the butter-soft leather sofa in front of the grand carved-stone fireplace.

"Make yourself comfortable." He offered her a knitted throw from a drawer. She shook her head.

He stroked it. "It's pure alpaca, from the mountains. Soft as the clouds that gather in the foothills." His sparkling gaze challenged her to resist.

"Well, if you put it that way." She let him drape it over her shoulders. Soft as a breath. And somehow the caress of his strong hands transmitted through the lush fabric.

She slipped her shoes off, and put them on the floor. When she looked up, the fire was already lit and blazing.

"How did you do that? It takes me half an hour to get a fire going." Sometimes even the fake logs sputtered out in her tiny apartment fireplace.

Amado shrugged. "Good kindling. Old wine barrels are the best." He smiled. "And we have a steady supply."

Without a word of warning, he seized her left foot and began to massage the sole with his broad thumb.

Susannah's mouth fell open.

Sometimes she was ticklish, but right now she had no urge to laugh. The penetrating motions of his thumb and fingers sent sensations ricocheting through her foot, up her leg and all over her body.

She should protest. This was far too intimate. But no words came to her mouth, and Amado just went about the task as if it was a service he provided to all guests.

He knelt at her feet. His dark hair hung in his eyes and she couldn't make out his expression. All she could see was the subtle movement of muscles in his bronzed forearms and powerful hands as he worked the day's tension—heck, the entire year's tension—out of her muscles with a deft, firm touch.

A long exhale escaped her.

"Ahh." Amado smiled as he looked up. His hands didn't even pause in their expert massage. "Now you're starting to relax."

His fingers worked his way up her instep and over her heel. Thank goodness she'd worn smart, silk panty hose.

"You take good care of your feet." Her sole buzzed deliciously as he went to work on the second foot. "They're strong and healthy."

Susannah laughed. "They'd better be with all I put them through."

"Tomorrow, we'll walk in the vineyards. You can stay tomorrow, can't you?" The sudden concern in his eyes tugged at something inside her. Why did he care if she stayed or went?

"I'll be here. I can't go home without your DNA. I could get fired."

Amado frowned and his fingers stopped their vigorous and soothing movements. "You'll get fired by the guy who's supposed to be my father? What kind of man is this?"

"A demanding one." She tried not to pay attention to the way he cradled her foot in his hands. "He expects the best from all his employees."

"Surely he can't fire you for something I've done, or rather, refused to do?"

"Sure he can. He'd see it as firing me for my failure to execute."

Amado looked thoughtful. Then he bent his head and resumed his precise massage. Susannah tried not to wriggle on the sofa as he nailed one pressure point after another, creating sensations of deep relaxation and startling pleasure.

She allowed herself to sink back into the cushions. To let go.

A night in Amado's bed in exchange for the DNA sample.

Her skin tingled at the prospect of those magic hands roaming…all over it. She suppressed a shiver of anticipation.

She was sure he'd keep the bargain. There was something old-world about him. He positively reeked of honor and integrity.

And sensuality. Their eyes met. Desire darkened his eyes and a spark of…something leaped between them.

Amado settled her feet gently on the ground. He rose and crossed the room.

She exhaled with relief as his intense and dangerously handsome presence receded into the shadows.

Spend the night in my bed.

His words from earlier—spoken half in jest, no doubt—seemed to hover in the air, thickening it. The crackling fire echoed the heat building and snapping inside her.

She hadn't made love in a long time.

Actually—not to put too fine a point on it—she hadn't made *love* ever. She'd had sex, but not for, oh…well, it was just plain embarrassing to think about how long it had been.

She was busy.

Always on the move.

Was there something wrong with having a sensual fling with an interested male? People did it all the time.

Her coworkers regaled their lurid exploits around the cappuccino machine in the office every Monday. Some of their stories made her jaw drop. They weren't saving themselves for Mr. Right any more than they had been in college. They lived for the moment.

They had fun.

Why couldn't she have some fun too, for a change?

Her ears pricked up at an exchange between Amado and Rosa. A minute later she heard Rosa leave, closing the door behind her.

She tensed in anticipation at the sound of Amado's decisive footsteps on the polished floor. He reappeared with two steaming white mugs.

And she'd get the DNA. Tarrant would be happy. She'd keep her job.

If Amado wasn't his son, which she suspected, there'd be no harm done.

If he was, Amado would no doubt inherit some of Tarrant's billions.

The retail tycoon was terminally ill and might have only

weeks to live. He was trying desperately to find and embrace his long-neglected, illegitimate offspring before he died.

Either way, she'd be doing a good deed.

Right?

Amado handed her a mug. His dark eyes narrowed. "You have a strange expression on your face."

"Me?" She let out a high, false laugh. "I'm just getting mesmerized by the fire, or something."

Emphasis on the *or something*.

She sniffed the contents of the cup. "Coffee at this time of night? Won't it keep us awake?"

Amado's mouth hitched slightly on one side. Something resembling a smile—or rather a wicked grin—crept across his face so slowly she wondered if she was imagining it. "Sometimes it's good to be awake at night."

He settled into the sofa beside her. Close. His muscled thigh brushed against her skirt.

Her pulse quickened.

The heat of his body mingled with the warmth of the fire and her own elevated body temperature.

What if Tarrant found out she'd slept with the man he thought was his son?

She swallowed hard. He wouldn't.

Amado would never tell. The old-world-honor thing. She sensed that he kept his emotions close to his chest. They'd spent hours together and while he'd talked about each of his wines like a beloved mistress, there'd been no mention whatsoever of his personal life.

She also suspected that—like his charming vineyard tour and his expert foot massage—he did this quite often.

Which, rather than alarming her, actually took the pressure off.

She sensed his steady dark gaze on her as she sipped her drink. Mmm. Sticky, rich, *dulce de leche* sweetened the coffee.

"Where does your family live now?"

His question jarred her out of the sensual fog she'd drifted into. "You mean my parents?"

He frowned. "Yes, and your brothers and sisters."

"I don't have any brothers and sisters. There's just me. My parents are back in the Philippines. They're running a program there for at-risk teens."

"They sound like good people."

"They are. I wish I was more like them. Or at least I feel I should wish that. But someone's got to devote their life to finding the best wines in the world, don't you think?"

Her words rang in the still air. Heat crept up her neck, embarrassment that she'd laid bare her insecurities.

Amado didn't blink. "Each of us has his or her own path. By trying to follow the wrong one, you do a disservice to yourself and to others." He laid a big, reassuring hand on her arm. "And I can't think of a more worthy pursuit than the quest for excellent wine." He tilted his head and his eyes glittered. "But then, I'm biased."

Her arm heated under his palm. He was close enough that she could smell his scent. She distracted herself by trying to analyze it.

Complex aroma, rich and appealing. A risky but invigorating blend of coffee, fermented grapes, burnt wood and hardworking male.

Full and robust bouquet. The finish might well be bittersweet…but worth it.

His palm moved over her forearm. Not really going anywhere, just moving back and forth. Stroking her.

She glanced at his face, but he didn't look up. He

seemed intent on the simple motion. Was this some kind of weird Argentine seduction trick?

If it was, it appeared to be working. Strange sensations bubbled inside her. When his hand slid to her thigh, resting lightly on it through the thin fabric of her skirt, it felt as natural and unthreatening as a handshake.

Or a kiss on the cheek.

Amado's lips brushed her cheekbone so lightly she wondered for a moment if she'd imagined it or simply wished it.

The second time his mouth rested for a moment right beside hers, until her lips stung with anticipation. His breath heated her skin.

His hand slid up her thigh, bringing her dress with it, until the hem climbed over her knee.

She realized she was leaning toward him. Since it felt so natural, she leaned closer, her nipples tight and tingling under her blousy top.

She slid one arm around him, aware of his muscled back through the soft fabric of his shirt.

Amado's bare palm on her thigh made her gasp. He'd hiked her skirt up almost to her underwear and warmth from the fire baked her skin.

She glanced at his face. His eyes were closed, his expression simple and familiar: the intense appreciation of a connoisseur.

Susannah's eyes slid shut as his mouth claimed hers, hot and ready. She could feel his body heat through their clothes. Almost without thinking, she pulled gently at his shirt until it came loose from his pants in the back, then she slid her fingers over the firm ridges of muscle on either side of his spine.

Excitement built inside her as their kiss deepened.

Heat gathered between her legs and desire thickened inside her.

It had been a long time since she'd kissed anyone. Usually she avoided personal entanglements. She was busy, she traveled a lot, and she didn't need the drama.

But this was perfect. They both knew what they wanted, and there was a neat and tidy ending already in sight.

Unless he was Tarrant's son, of course. A frisson of unease rippled through her.

But that was unlikely. With his dark coloring and smooth, sculpted features, Amado didn't look like the angular, blue-eyed Tarrant. And Clara certainly didn't fit the mold of Tarrant's glamorous ex-lovers.

She shoved the potential complication from her mind.

Tonight would be a delicious interlude. A sweet taste of pleasure, like the sip of a wine she knew she wouldn't buy for the company, but that she drank purely for her own enjoyment.

Amado cupped her breast in his broad hand, strumming her nipple until it peaked against his palm.

"Come with me," he breathed the words in her ear.

He picked up her hand and squeezed it in his. Anticipation shone in his coffee-brown eyes.

She rose from the sofa, legs shivering. Her whole body tingled with arousal, from her scalp to the soles of her well-massaged feet.

He led her by the hand, the perfect gentleman, except that he was doing something a perfect gentleman would never do—seduce a virtual stranger.

Somehow that gave her an illicit thrill.

She'd always been the good girl, the minister's daughter no one even dared to look at, let alone entice into bed. She'd been taught from toddlerhood to set a good example for those around her. To think about others and put her own needs aside.

For a long time, she never even knew she had needs.

Right now, as her belly throbbed with desire, she was aware of little else.

Three

Amado led Susannah past antique furniture and rugs glowing with the rich colors of natural pigments. The house had obviously been lovingly cared for by generations of grateful owners.

The stairway's curved wood banister gleamed in the distant firelight. They exchanged a cautious smile.

Well, hers was cautious, his was encouraging.

Come into my chamber, said the spider to the fly.

But she was a willing fly, so why not?

Amado's personal bedchamber was large, with velvet floor-length draperies covering the windows. A four-poster bed carved from dark wood dominated the space. The fluffy white duvet covered the high mattress like a low-hanging cloud, inviting Susannah to sink into its softness.

Amado rested his hand on her hip. He kissed her with exquisite gentleness, taking his time, savoring her.

She let her fingers roam over his shirt, enjoying the shape of him beneath the fabric. His body was hard and athletic, capable of speed and force. But his movements were tender, almost unbearably so, as he licked her lips, brushed them with his mouth, and nuzzled his cheek gently against hers.

His suntanned skin wasn't exactly soft, but it wasn't rough either. Everything about Amado seemed smooth and mellow, like a fine wine.

He pulled back slightly. "Let me make you at home in my bed."

Her insides shimmered at the prospect. Amado's dark eyes shone with simple desire that echoed her own. His forearms brushed the sides of her breasts, stirring delicious tremors of sensation, as he unhooked and unzipped the back of her dress.

He lowered the fabric over her shoulders to reveal her bra. She'd worn a pretty one today. Had she somehow known?

His big hands cupped the silver-gray satin and lace, and rubbed her nipples gently through the fabric. Susannah couldn't help wriggling as arousal tingled over her skin. She reached for his shirt and pulled the buttons out through the soft fabric.

Amado's chest was thickly muscled, with a narrow trail of hair descending from his belly button into the low-slung waist of his pants. A sturdy leather belt held the latter firmly closed, and she struggled with the stiff hide while Amado layered hot, breathy kisses over her neck.

His erection jutted beneath the buckle. She enjoyed a naughty sense of satisfaction at this proof that he was every bit as turned on and wound up as she was.

At last, she pulled the leather loose and tackled the fly

of his pants. As she pushed the khaki fabric down over his hard thighs, her fingers trembled with excitement.

Amado eased her dress down, and squeezed her backside. His eyes were closed, his lips slightly parted. He had a wide mouth with a bold, sensual cut. High cheekbones and a strong nose. The kind of looks that made women sigh and nudge each other.

Susannah was usually intimidated by extravagant good looks in a man. She didn't want to deal with the oversize ego that came with them.

But with Amado, his proud features seemed a natural extension of everything she admired and liked about him: his passion and dedication, the confidence born of hard-won success.

Why shouldn't you be arrogant, if you'd earned the right?

He unhooked the clasp on the front of her bra, and lifted the cups from her breasts. Tight with arousal, her nipples stung in the night air drifting through the open windows.

He eased the straps down over her arms, and placed her bra carefully on a chair, on top of her neatly folded dress.

With the same careful deliberation he lowered his head and licked her left nipple. The rough texture of his tongue on the supersensitive flesh made her gasp. At the same moment, he slid his fingers into her panties. She could feel herself slick against them.

Should she be embarrassed that her arousal was so obvious? She didn't know what to think. Couldn't think, as pleasure stole over her body.

Amado's delight in her was palpable. She could sense his heart beating beneath his ribs, hear his deepening breaths as he sucked her nipples to peaks of pleasurable tension.

He eased her panties down over her thighs and placed them on the chair, then removed his underwear and stood facing her. They watched each other. Both naked, aroused, expectant.

His sturdy male body and the raw strength it implied appealed to her in a way she couldn't begin to articulate or even understand.

But why should she? She didn't need to analyze everything and understand it. She didn't need to figure out how it all fit together.

"You see the world differently than other people."

Amado's low voice crept into her ear.

She blinked. "How?" Could he read her thoughts?

She felt naked. She *was* naked.

He stroked her chin. "You don't see only the surface of things. You see inside them, too."

"I'm not so sure. I don't see inside you."

His dark eyes fixed on hers.

"Yes, you do."

She frowned. What did he think she was thinking? Should she ask? Her heart beat faster.

But she didn't get a chance to ask because Amado's bold mouth covered hers in a swift and forceful kiss.

At the same time, he swept her into his arms as if she weighed nothing and laid her on the duvet.

She sank into the thick, soft surface and Amado climbed over her. For a second, she wondered if he'd part her legs and enter her, and her belly tightened with a mix of fear and anticipation.

But he didn't. He stretched himself out alongside her, skin to skin, his flat stomach against her hip, his long, hard thighs against hers, his muscled arm holding her close.

"Welcome home." He nuzzled her ear and kissed her neck.

Susannah's eyes widened as a powerful and deeply strange sensation flooded her.

Welcome home? What a weird thing to say. Still, no reason to get all worked up. It was probably his shtick for the tourists. It wasn't like he actually *meant* it.

"Your brain is so busy," he whispered. "Sometimes you just have to be."

"To be what?" Her brain raced faster.

"You."

"And who's that?"

He kissed her ear, his warm breath sending shivers of heat dancing through her. "Just you."

His gaze shone black in the scant silver moonlight creeping in around the draperies. "Your mouth." He licked her lips, left them cool and humming.

"Your neck." He bit it gently, a careful vampire.

"Your chest." He brushed her breast with his cheek, then sucked each nipple in turn.

"Your stomach." He blew hot air on her skin, making it shiver. Then he licked around her belly button and grazed her skin with his teeth. For a second, her womb seemed to yearn toward him and Susannah almost cried out from the odd and powerful sensation.

Maybe Suki was right to warn her about Argentine men. She'd never experienced anything like this before. Her previous sexual experience was a series of quick and embarrassed fumbles by comparison.

And they hadn't even done anything yet.

"Stop thinking."

Her insides contracted again, and ripples of pleasure washed through her.

What is this man doing to me?

He parted her legs and lowered his mouth between her thighs. He licked and sucked until her hips rose off the mattress and a high-pitched moan escaped her mouth.

Her eyes flew open and she glanced down to see his gaze gleaming in the moonlight.

"Just let go and be. With me." His voice rasped, husky. His hair fell to his eyes, which fixed on her, dark slits of passion.

Already half insane with arousal, Susannah wriggled against him, enjoying the sensation of his hot, hungry mouth on her flesh. Fierce contractions rocked her, starting from his tongue—like the plug in an electric socket—and surging through her entire body in waves. They flung her against the bed where she cried out, again and again, as Amado moved his mouth over her, rocking her deeper into the crazy otherworld where there was no thought, only fierce and overwhelming pleasure.

Howling outside the windows penetrated her consciousness as her shuddering body collapsed back against the hot duvet.

"What's that?" she gasped.

"The dogs." Amado grinned. "They want to know what all the fuss is about."

Her hand flew to her mouth. She could hear them yowling outside the window. "Did I make that much noise?"

"Yes." He nuzzled her neck, his pleasure at her abandon written all over his face. "But don't start thinking now."

"I don't know what…I've never…" Susannah frowned. Stray energy still whipped through her in uneven bursts.

"You never had an orgasm?"

"Is that what this is?"

Amado grinned. "Sure is. Feels good, huh?"

Susannah nodded.

Amado bent down and kissed her belly, which contracted tightly as his lips touched her. "You're sensitive." He looked up, eyes shining. "Very responsive."

He leaned away from her and she heard him rip something. He turned and rolled a condom over his impressive erection. Susannah blinked.

He was so...matter-of-fact about it. Unembarrassed. Like this was a normal, everyday thing to do.

Maybe it was, for him.

He climbed over her and her skin tingled as he hovered above her. He nuzzled her neck again—how she loved that—and breathed in her ear. "You feel more than other people. That's why you think too much. But it's okay to simply feel."

Susannah swallowed. Her brain wanted to make sense of his words but her body was utterly focused on Amado. He entered her in a single swift motion that pushed her into the soft mattress.

So aroused already, she couldn't stop herself from climaxing again immediately. Tremors rippled through her. She could hear the sounds she was making, but she couldn't do anything about them. Couldn't prevent her arms from winding around his powerful torso and clutching him close.

"Oh, Amado." She heard herself cry out his name as he moved inside her. He thrust into her, gentle, then harder, slow, then fast. Taking his time, then rushing until she climaxed again—and again—totally unable to control the spasm of her muscles and the shivering sneezes of sensation that racked her body.

She took him deeper, pleading with him in Spanish and in English and several other languages to take her and love her and hold her and make her his. To go faster and rougher and harder and...

Amado shouted as he climaxed. She opened her eyes in time to see his face in tortured ecstasy. He held her so tight she could barely breathe and they crashed into the mattress together with force. He panted, hugging her to him, moaning, as he throbbed inside her.

"Por amor." His breath rasped against her ear.

Susannah blinked, blinded by even the tiny slivers of moonlight that played across the walls. *Love?*

It was probably just an expression. She didn't know Argentine idioms.

Besides, her mind didn't seem to work too well anymore. She was all body. All sensation, all touch and lick and soft, pliant wetness.

Amado's head lay on her chest—he appeared to have collapsed from exhaustion, but she could see his eyes on her, wide and dark and filled with…amazement.

Susannah blew out a breath. The first hint of rational thought came sneaking back.

What the heck happened to you?

Had she really been yelping and panting so loud that she set the dogs off?

A flush spread over her already hot and sticky face.

As if they'd been listening, the dogs let out a chorus of enthusiastic barks.

Stray shards of the things she'd said—that she'd moaned and shouted—popped into her mind. Local idioms she'd learned over the years while being instructed *never* to use them under any circumstances. Words that had apparently lodged in her subconscious waiting for just this moment to make their appearance.

Amado still stared at her. Barely blinking.

"Are you okay?" Her words sounded oddly clinical in the thick lush silence of the night.

"No," he breathed. "I'm much, much, much, better than okay." He swallowed. "You?"

The words appeared to cost him great effort. How long

had they been…Susannah bit her lip. It could have been hours. The poor man was exhausted.

Or was he? She thought she detected a sudden wicked gleam in his eye.

"You are a woman of many dimensions, Susannah Clarke."

Far more than I'd previously suspected.

Susannah wasn't sure it was a good thing to be capable of such total sexual abandon. Seemed the kind of trait that could get you into trouble.

At least her secret would be safe with Amado. Tierra de Oro was very far from New York. And surely no one would ever get her going like that again.

Thank goodness.

Amado's breathing slowed and steadied. His muscles relaxed and grew heavier, as he pulled her closer to him. He shifted slightly, and let out a sigh.

He'd fallen asleep—on her.

Susannah couldn't help a burst of silent laughter, and even the vibration of her chest didn't stir him. He looked so sweet lying there, his handsome face nestled between her breasts and his arms wrapped securely around her torso.

Apparently he was quite at home with her in his bed. And why wouldn't he be? She had no illusions that this was a rare occasion for him. He was gorgeous and an incorrigible flirt. She really didn't even mind.

Did she?

She swallowed.

Didn't want to think about that.

In a day or so she'd be back in New York, updating her database and checking on the deliveries she was expecting from vineyards all around the world.

Including Amado's. Some of his wines were daring and successful to the point where she was sure Tarrant would want them for his own cellars.

Which meant she'd still have to deal with Amado.

Or not? Amado concerned himself with the aspects of the business that interested him, the hands-on growing and fermenting. He left the marketing and shipping to his capable staff.

Most likely she'd chat on the phone with a friendly assistant who'd give her the advertising spiel on the various wines and send her samples and...

Samples.

She couldn't leave here without the DNA sample.

Susannah swallowed hard.

I'll give you a sample of my DNA—just to prove that you're wrong, of course—if you'll spend the night in my bed.

She'd held up her end of the bargain.

But somehow, asking for his DNA now would be harder than ever.

Four

Susannah snuck out of Amado's bed and back into her own room sometime before dawn. She needed to compose herself and regain her professional demeanor—or what was left of it—before she confronted him again.

His enormous white dogs greeted the sunrise with a chorus of enthusiastic baying. Heat crept up her neck when she heard the sound.

She dressed carefully in a plain black dress and arranged her hair into a chignon. It was too tangled to wear down. Her lips were red from kissing and she tried to tone down her flushed cheeks with loose powder.

There wasn't anything she could do about the dazzled look in her eyes.

When she heard Rosa arrive in a car and start clattering around in the kitchen, Susannah took a deep breath and went downstairs, determined to act as if nothing had happened. Her offer to help was politely rebuffed so she sat in front of the unlit fireplace.

When breakfast was ready, Rosa yelled up to Amado. Susannah rose from the sofa and held her breath as his door creaked open.

Amado appeared, sleepy and disheveled, at the top of the stairs. He stopped when he saw her. Susannah swallowed as he rested his eyes on her and a smile spread over his face. He eased down the stairs on bare feet.

"Morning," he whispered. His eyes had the same dazed look she'd seen in her own mirror that morning.

His pale blue shirt hung unbuttoned, revealing an enticing slice of tanned chest.

"Hi," she stuttered. Then she refocused her eyes on the door to the dining room, blinked, and attempted to guide her feet in that direction.

Rosa tutted at the sight of Amado. He simply smiled at her.

He pulled out a chair for Susannah. "Sit down. Eat."

Susannah snuck a glance at Rosa, whose stolid face was characteristically expressionless.

Did Amado always eat breakfast half dressed?

Or only when he'd slept with his guest the previous night. No need to stand on ceremony when you'd spent the night writhing and moaning in each other's arms.

She fanned her napkin out over her lap. She had nothing to be ashamed of. They were both adults and she…

Rosa's withering look made her shrink into her chair.

Amado didn't even bother to make polite conversation. Relaxed and at ease, he enjoyed the breakfast Rosa had prepared for them.

Susannah wanted to concentrate on her creamy *café con leche* and the delicious fresh baked rolls and pastries with homemade jam, but it was hard with Amado sitting across the table, staring right at her.

He caught her gaze time after time, his dark eyes shining with pleasure, until her heart was ready to flutter right out of her chest.

I've got to get out of here, was the thought foremost in her mind. Amado had an unhealthy and dangerous effect on her libido.

She was here to do a job. She was actually being paid for this, and she'd better start to earn her salary—if she wanted to keep it, that is.

She checked that Rosa was out of earshot.

Her heart thudded as she leaned forward. "You will give me the DNA, won't you?"

Amado's expression hardened. The smile slipped from his mouth and faded from his eyes. "Yes."

A chill descended over the breakfast table. He pulled his napkin from his lap and rose to his feet. Padded silently away, leaving her sitting, staring after him.

She kept her breathing steady and forced a smile as the grim Rosa came back into the room with more coffee. "No, thanks."

Right now, she felt guilty eating their food and enjoying their hospitality. What if Tarrant Hardcastle was right, and she was about to show them all that Amado was the illegitimate product of a casual affair?

Amado buttoned his shirt and slicked his hair back with a comb. He had a bizarre sensation of going into battle.

Susannah Clarke was here to impugn his mother's name. Of course, the idea that his mother had an affair was preposterous, so he wasn't afraid of the test results. Still, his cheerful mood had evaporated.

So, she'd slept with him for purely practical purposes. Why did that bother him? He'd slept with her for his own reasons, which admittedly were far less complicated.

Had no idea what he was getting into, either. He'd never met a woman like this. So cool and composed on the outside, so fiery and abandoned in his bed. Fascinating.

Then this morning she confronted him with that prim smile. Reminded him that last night's enjoyment was simply part of a cold-blooded business deal for her.

Irritation spiked in his gut as he buckled his belt. Still, he was a man of honor, and he'd made a promise.

He heard her moving about in the guest bedroom, and he entered without knocking. "My body is yours to do with as you like."

She dropped whatever she was packing in her bag and looked up. She looked nervous, so slender and delicate in her long black dress.

He cocked his head. "Did I startle you?"

She blinked and swallowed. Nervous. "I'm just getting my things together."

"I can see that. So what's the plan? You extract my bodily fluids and head back to New York with them?" His eyes narrowed as a nasty thought crept over his brain. "Or did you already take what you were looking for?"

Susannah swallowed. "No! I didn't take anything." She colored. "There's a lab in Mendoza that can process the test. It would be best if you come there with me so they can take the sample themselves. That way there's less risk of contamination, and you'll be sure that no one, you know, tampered with..."

She trailed off and tucked an imaginary lock behind her ear. A strange gesture since her long dark hair was secured in a tight chignon. Her dress buttoned to her neck and flared from the waist almost to her ankles.

She looked every inch the prudish missionary's daughter.

Touch me not.

But he knew better.

"So you want me to accompany you into Mendoza?"

"Well, I'd imagine you'd need to bring your own car..."

"So you don't have to drive me home again." He tilted his head. "You think of all the details."

"And actually," her hands trembled as she struggled with the zipper of her bag, "I ran out of gas on my way here so, I'm afraid I'll need some before I can go anywhere."

Amado crossed his arms. "It appears that once again you are at my mercy. Lucky thing I'm a gentleman." A wicked smile crept over his lips. "At least some of the time."

Her lips parted and she looked like she wanted to protest. He shouldn't toy with her this way. She was obviously rather innocent and unschooled when it came to men, and she didn't deserve to be teased.

Still, she had slept with him. She was a grown-up. She knew what she was doing.

And now they both knew she had a wild side.

That intrigued him more than he could say. What other secrets hid beneath that that cool and demure exterior?

Since Amado didn't fancy cramming himself into her tiny rental car, they took his Mercedes sedan and arranged for one of his employees to drive her car back to town and meet him later.

During the drive, they talked easily about the area and its history and Amado's family. He got a strong sense that she didn't believe he was this Hardcastle man's son, either.

"Will your boss be upset when you don't bring back the results he's expecting?"

"I can't see how he could be. Honestly, I don't know anything about how they're finding people or what they want. I do know he's dying, though."

"From what?"

"Prostate cancer. He wouldn't mind me telling you. He and his wife have been active in trying to encourage people to get tested and seek treatment early. He says he ignored his symptoms for too long because he thought he was invincible."

Amado frowned. The illness made this foreign stranger seem more real to him. "Is he suffering?"

"I'd imagine so. No one wants to die." She looked out the window, to where the Andes rose in the distance. "This quest to find his lost children is keeping him going, from what I hear. It's become a passion for him."

"But why does he want to find them?"

"I think he wants to confront his past mistakes, or failings, or something. Face up to them before he dies."

"So he thinks I'm one of his past *mistakes?*" Amado couldn't help laughing.

"It does sound rude, put like that. He's very rich, though. I suspect he wants to leave some of his vast fortune to them."

She looked at him with those dark, perceptive eyes. Studying him for signs of greed?

Fifteen years ago, even five years ago, money might have been welcome as he tried to bring the *estancia* up to modern methods of production. The construction of the state-of-the-art winery had involved large and complicated loans.

But now the vineyard was humming and prosperous.

The last of the debts had been paid three years ago and they were seeing comfortable profit margins.

"I don't want his money or anyone else's. Unless they're buying my wine, of course."

For most of the drive, though, they didn't talk about Tarrant Hardcastle at all. Susannah seemed to be enchanted by the beauty of the region. Once in the city, she marveled at the open ditches bringing water down from the mountains to irrigate the many trees and fountains. Amado explained the technique had been in use by the Huarpe people when the Spanish settlers first arrived, and it was the same system of *aquecias* that made lush vineyards possible today despite the low annual rainfall.

The lab was on a quiet side street. Amado could tell Susannah was jittery as they pulled into a parking space. She laughed and exclaimed as he led her over one of the neat ditches that lined the city sidewalks. What did she stand to gain or lose from all of this?

For her, it was a purely professional matter. However the results came out, she'd done her duty and could wash her hands of the situation.

Of him.

His muscles tightened with an uncomfortable mixture of irritation and longing. It infuriated him that she could spend the night with him—and such a night—then just walk away.

She spoke quietly to the person behind the counter, prim and proper in her black dress with its row of buttons down the back.

He couldn't help wanting to unbutton them, one by one, and expose her smooth, olive skin. To lick the delicate bumps of her spine and layer soft kisses over her waist…

He shoved a hand through his hair. No sense getting all worked up. He wasn't required to donate sperm.

"Come this way." A uniformed nurse—or someone dressed like a nurse—ushered them through a door behind the reception desk. This whole situation gave him the creeps.

Who knew what they were going to do with his private biological information? Maybe he'd end up accused of some crime or discover he carried the gene for a terminal illness.

"Sit here, sir."

He lowered himself into the plastic chair and held his head high as the nurse stuck a long cotton swab into this mouth and rubbed it against his cheek. "All done."

"That's it?" he asked, adrenaline pumping.

That's all it took to change a life? To ruin it, even? It didn't seem right.

Still, he knew what the results would say. No reason to worry.

He looked at Susannah, slim and lovely and nervous as a hungry cat, twisting her fingers and toying with the skirt of her dress.

The nurse left the room with the sample.

Amado didn't take his eyes off Susannah. "Let's go eat lunch."

"I should head for the airport. I need to get back to New York."

So easy for her to just leave. Clearly, leaving was part of her modus operandi in life. Dust off her hands, and move on.

He wasn't ready for her to leave yet. "You can't go until we have the results."

"Why not?"

"Because I might pay off the lab to get the results I want." He narrowed his eyes.

"You couldn't. They have a stellar reputation."

He cocked his head. "Any man, or woman…has their price." He glanced meaningfully at the door. Which opened to admit the brisk blond nurse.

"All under way. We should have results in five days."

"Five days?" Amado rose to his feet, almost knocking over the chair.

"That's our minimum period of time for accurate analysis." The nurse shuffled a stack of papers. "We'll call and let you know when the results are in."

Amado glared at Susannah. She was heading back to her ordinary life and leaving him to deal with the fallout from the tests. Resentment tangled with unspent desire in his chest.

"What time is your plane?"

"I'll take the first plane I can board to Santiago, Chile. My flight for New York leaves from there tonight." Susannah followed the nurse out the door into the waiting area.

"You had your ticket booked the whole time? You must have been very sure of getting your sample."

The nurse glanced back at him. Most likely she thought Susannah was collecting his DNA to prove paternity of their child. It rankled him that anyone could think of him as the kind of cad who'd dispute such a thing.

"I was hopeful." Susannah avoided his glance as she thanked the receptionist and paid by credit card.

Of course, she couldn't have suspected he'd persuade her to sleep with him.

Could she?

A growing sense of panic gripped Susannah as Amado pulled into a parking space at the airport.

He lifted her suitcase from the trunk. "You'll come back when the new Malbec is ready?" He looked toward the terminal as if he didn't care one way or the other.

Likely it would be an inconvenience for him if she came back. Awkward and embarrassing. He'd have enjoyed several more encounters with visiting females by then. Possibly he'd have forgotten her.

She didn't want to look like she cared, either.

"I'd love to, but I'm afraid it depends upon my schedule. I have a series of trips to Europe and South Africa over the upcoming months."

She did her best to sound businesslike, talking about Tierra de Oro's projected production and Hardcastle's possible orders. Of course, she had no idea if any of it would come to fruition. Likely the DNA test and its resultant emotional fall out would determine Tarrant's order one way or the other.

Did she regret what she'd done?

A little. She had a strange sense of having unleashed a genie. Exciting but scary.

Amado's dark eyes still shone with desire. No doubt her own did, too.

Desire wasn't something you could control. You could choose not to act on it, but you couldn't make it go away.

If you did act on it, you could end up like Tarrant Hardcastle with a host of unplanned children and a lifetime of complications.

Misgivings tightened her muscles. She had a strange feeling she'd never forget her night with Amado. How would she feel now, alone in her bed, tormented by memories of intimacy and passion she could never have imagined?

At the security check-in, he held her face between his hands and kissed her full on the mouth. Arousal kicked through her as his tongue danced with hers right there in line at the ticket counter, surrounded by the swirling, impatient crowds.

Don't think you'll get off so easy, his kiss seemed to say.

Her mouth throbbed as he pulled back. Her stomach clenched and she wobbled on her heels.

Triumph glittered in Amado's eyes. Then he frowned. "You'll call me with the results?"

A cool shiver crept down her spine. "I suspect someone from Tarrant's office will call you. I don't usually have anything to do with his private business. I'm just here as an envoy."

"An envoy of distressing news. You're brave."

"Or desperate to keep my job." She attempted levity. "You can't say no to Tarrant Hardcastle. But I doubt they'll even tell me the results."

Amado's frown deepened. "I'll tell you."

That reassurance of future contact made her heart swell. The thought of just…leaving and never seeing him again was too grim to contemplate.

She was sure he'd call her to laugh and joke if the result was what he hoped for.

But if it wasn't?

Susannah pretended to fumble with her ticket as Amado turned and strode away. She couldn't help turning to catch a last glimpse of him as he disappeared through the door.

So tall and proud and strong, his passion evident in everything he did. His connection to the estate and his family so deep as to be unquestionable.

She chewed a manicured fingernail and hoped like hell that Tarrant was wrong.

Susannah's heart thundered as she climbed the wide, polished stairs to the El Cubano cigar bar on Manhattan's Fifth Avenue. One week had passed since her return from Argentina, and Tarrant Hardcastle had summoned her to his exclusive watering hole to thank her for retrieving—his word—Amado's DNA.

She had no idea what the results were. But would he ask her here if the trip had been a waste of time?

She gave her coat to the stunning coat-check girl and followed the maître d' into the hushed space. The lack of cigar smoke surprised her, since men sat all around, sunk deep into leather chairs, with expensive bundles of rolled leaves burning in their hands.

On the far side of the room they reached the imposing backs of a pair of chairs arranged in front of a window. The leather thrones enjoyed a spectacular view over Fifth Avenue.

"Mr. Hardcastle, your guest has arrived."

Susannah sucked in a smoke-free breath as her boss rose and greeted her. Even rows of white teeth shone in his tanned face.

He was disturbingly youthful-looking for sixty-seven, in a way that could not be entirely natural.

Everything about the man was frightening.

She tried not to wince or fall over as he kissed her on both cheeks. An extravagant gesture of greeting for a boss she barely saw.

"Thank you, my dear." His blue-green eyes glittered with emotion.

Uh-oh.

"Thank you for finding my son."

Susannah's mouth fell open and her stomach plummeted.

"He is your son?" she rasped.

"Ninety-nine-point-nine percent certain. It doesn't get more definite than that." He gestured at the plush leather armchair opposite his. "Sit."

Susannah practically fell into it.

Tarrant summoned a waiter with a wave of his hand.

"Tell me about him, my dear. My son, what is he like?" A beaming smile lit his tanned face as he settled back into his chair.

Amado isn't the son of Ignacio Alvarez. His mother had an affair.

The reality of the situation chilled her blood. How had Amado reacted? How had his parents reacted? He hadn't called her with the news, as he'd promised.

"He's nice," she stammered. "Very smart."

Tarrant waved his hand impatiently. "Does he look like me?"

Susannah frowned. "You both have strong features. I can see a resemblance around the nose and cheekbones. He's darker, though, with dark eyes and hair."

Tarrant smiled. "Like my son Dominic. I never could resist the allure of a dark young beauty, back then."

Susannah tried not to recoil. Tarrant's steady gaze made her uncomfortably conscious of her own dark coloring. She *so* did not want to think about Tarrant's sexual exploits of thirty-odd years ago.

It was downright hard to imagine Clara Alvarez being a beauty, dark or otherwise. Didn't she have blue eyes like Tarrant?

"His mother was such a stunner. Sharp as a cracked whip and with a fire that…" He blew out a breath and shook his head.

"Clara is well and healthy, too."

"Clara?" Tarrant sipped a clear drink. Martini probably. "Who's that?"

"Amado's mother."

Tarrant put his drink down. "Amado's mother is dead." A chill crept up her spine. "But I met her."

"Hardly. I was called to identify the body."

Susannah swallowed hard. Her blood seemed to stop flowing. "But he called her 'mother.'"

"I don't know who the heck Clara is, but his real mother was Marisa Alvarez and she died giving birth to her son." He tapped his cigar. "Tragic. The whole situation was a nightmare."

Susannah blinked, unable to make sense of it.

Amado very definitely believed himself to be the son of Clara and Ignacio Alvarez. Now he wasn't related to either of them?

Tarrant studied the end of his cigar. "My son, Amado, will unfortunately not return my calls."

"How did he learn the news?"

"My daughter Fiona managed to get him on the phone long enough to share the happy news, but he hung up on her. She's not terribly subtle, but I had hoped that the blood ties would..."

He let out a long sigh. "I'm truly impressed that you managed to coax him into providing a sample." His eyes narrowed. "You're a quiet one, and I can tell there's more to you than meets the eye."

Susannah shrank into her chair, feeling guilty.

"So I need you to go back to Argentina and bring my son home."

Icy shock rushed over her. *Back to Tierra de Oro?* "You want me to *bring him* to New York?"

"I need to meet him. To show him the business. To welcome him to his place in it."

A sharp flash of adrenaline stung her muscles at the prospect of seeing Amado again. Then reality set in. Tarrant wanted his son to join the business like his other newfound son Dominic.

Her stomach clenched and she recoiled at the prospect

of trying to convince Amado to leave the home he loved so much. No matter how much money was involved, that would be *wrong*.

"He'll never leave the *estancia*." The words flew from her tongue. "It's everything to him, his life's work. He loves it like…" *Like a father loves his son.*

She held her tongue. Regretted the passion with which she'd spoken.

Tarrant frowned and studied her. "Bring him here just long enough to meet his old man before I die."

Susannah blinked. No doubt he was confident that once he got Amado in his reaches he could talk him into anything.

Tarrant was such a force of nature it was easy to forget he was dying of cancer. The disease was so advanced that his doctors had advised him to avoid debilitating treatments and to enjoy his last months—or weeks—as best he could. Already he'd outlived their predictions.

Pity trickled through her, despite her misgivings. "I don't know if he'll come. It was hard to persuade him to part with the sample."

"I know you can do it. My assistant has booked you a flight to Santiago this evening. You'll be back in Mendoza by morning."

"But I'm supposed to fly to Johannesburg tomorrow." She had eleven vineyard tours lined up.

His face closed over. "Johannesburg can wait. *I* can't. You must bring him here this week. At once."

Susannah opened her mouth to protest—then closed it again.

This was her boss. Everyone knew the company was his personal fiefdom and if he wanted her to cancel a week's worth of carefully planned tours to go on a personal errand, she'd better do it.

"Reassure him that the visit will be worth his while." Tarrant leaned forward, resting a gray-suited elbow on his chair. "Despite my reputation, I'm not such an egotist that I believe everyone on earth knows who I am. Tell him who I am. What I can give him."

The emotion on his face surprised her. She was seeing another side to Tarrant Hardcastle. Under the brash tycoon exterior was a human being, fragile and insecure like everyone else. A man who wanted to meet the son he fathered before it was too late. Who maybe even craved affection and love that he'd forsaken for so long.

Her heart squeezed. She had to help him.

He grabbed her hand. "I'm a dying man. Don't be afraid to tug at his heartstrings." He squeezed, his bony fingertips pressing into her palm. "All men have them, despite what we'd prefer you women to believe."

Five

Susannah, exhausted almost to the point of collapse, pulled into the driveway of Tierra de Oro the following afternoon.

She'd rented a larger car with a bigger fuel tank as a measure of self-preservation. But the way she felt right now, if Amado's huge white dogs wanted to eat her alive, they were quite welcome.

She hadn't called. Tarrant had been sure the element of surprise was in her favor and she suspected he was right.

She'd jumped a foot into the air every time her phone rang in the last twenty-four hours. But Amado hadn't called her either, despite his promise.

She parked in front of the house. Inhaled deeply. Then she summoned her last ounce of strength to tug on the door handle, and stepped out into the blinding sun.

The first thing she heard was the high-pitched keening of a woman weeping.

Uh-oh.

She approached the door, wincing at the loud crunch of her shoes on the gravel drive.

Heart pounding, she knocked. Held herself steady as footsteps approached. The tall wood-paneled door flung open.

Amado.

For a second his face was blank with shock. Then his fierce black gaze hit her like a blast from a shotgun. "You."

She swallowed hard. "Me."

He was taller and more imposing than she remembered. More handsome, too. His hair hung in his eyes and made him look slightly wild. Uncivilized.

"Look what you've done." His fierce whisper grated on her ears. He gestured inside the house. Racking sobs filled the serene, antique-filled space. "My mother is distraught."

A strange expression came over his face.

She's not your mother.

She kept silent as the thought passed between them, thickening the tension in the air.

The two big white dogs appeared, sentries at Amado's sides. Their dark eyes peered up at her as if to ask "Why?"

Susannah took a step backward, and almost fell off the steps. Amado leaped forward and pulled her roughly back up.

Then he tugged his hand away as if the bare skin of her arm had stung him like a jellyfish.

"Thank you," she stammered. "I'm sorry, I didn't mean to hurt you or your family…"

His eyes narrowed. "But you had a job to do." She could hear the controlled rage in his deep voice.

She swallowed.

Another loud wail rang through the air.

Amado forced a grim smile. Gestured into the pain-filled interior. "Why don't you come in?"

He disappeared into the cool gloom of the house. One of the dogs shot her an accusatory look over his powerful shoulders before following obediently at his master's heels.

Every muscle in her body itched with the urge to turn and flee. But her parents had taught her to cope with tough situations, not run from them.

Susannah inhaled a shaky breath and stepped inside.

Clara Alvarez sat on the sofa, head in her hands. Sobs racked her solid body.

"Mamá." Amado spoke softly.

"I'm not your mother." Her meaty hands muffled the tear-thickened words. "I shouldn't have played a part in this charade. I lied. God will curse me. I deserve to suffer." Her fresh howl of pain ripped a hole in Susannah's gut.

What on earth had happened here thirty-one years ago?

Amado shook his head.

"She's so upset. My father has ridden off into the mountains. He won't speak to anyone."

He strode across the room, and Susannah followed, hoping to get out of earshot of the distraught Clara. Tension hummed in the air, and in her own anxious body. The *estancia*'s tranquil, nurturing atmosphere had been shattered. Possibly forever.

"Can we go out on the terrace?" she whispered.

Amado frowned at her, but opened the door and ushered her out.

The sun glared at them over jagged mountain peaks that suddenly looked like the teeth of a giant saw.

Susannah steadied herself. The situation really couldn't get any worse. Now seemed as good a time as any to blurt out her request. "Your real father wants you to come to New York."

"My *real father*." The words tore from Amado's lips like

a foul curse. "How can you say that? A strange man who cared nothing for me. Who abandoned me to fate. Now he seeks to claim me for reasons of his own and doesn't care whose life he ruins in the process."

"He's very sorry for how he treated his lost children." Susannah twisted her hands together.

"Lost? I wasn't lost. I was at home here in Tierra de Oro." Pain shone in his eyes. "The estate has passed from father to son, for six generations. Now the chain is broken because my father has no son."

He broke off and stared out at the mountains.

The acres of lush vineyards sprawled in a rich, striped carpet below them. The grapes no doubt growing and ripening, regardless of the human drama inside the house.

Susannah could hardly bring herself to look at Amado's strained profile. "I don't understand. Who was Marisa Alvarez?"

He didn't turn to face her. "Marisa Alvarez was my sister."

Susannah's hand flew to her mouth. "A sister? I didn't know you had one."

"Why would you? She's been dead for thirty years." Now he turned. His dark gaze burned her. "And she wasn't my sister at all."

Susannah blinked, sure anything she could say would be worse than nothing. She couldn't make sense of what he was saying.

She wanted to offer him something, maybe even a reassuring hand. But his rigid posture and proud expression prevented her.

She could still remember the powerful sensation of being held in his strong arms. Lying in his bed, suffused with pleasure and spent tension, more relaxed than she'd ever been in her life.

That felt like a lifetime ago.

"Marisa, my sister, lived a quiet life here at Tierra de Oro. Her mother—Ignacio's first wife—died in childbirth, so she was raised by her widowed father."

He glanced at her. "I knew all this. What I didn't know is that, when Marisa was seventeen, she grew tired of being sheltered and protected by her father. After spending a summer studying art in Mendoza, and secretly earning money from selling her paintings, she ran away to New York."

Susannah blew out a breath. It was starting to make sense.

"My father," he raised an eyebrow, "or should I say Ignacio, knows little about this part of her life. But she stayed there for over a year and during that time she met Tarrant Hardcastle."

His words dripped with venom at the name.

"And they had an affair," Susannah whispered.

"Yes. And she got pregnant. At which point he told her to get rid of it or he was done with her."

Susannah winced.

Amado blew out a hard breath and shook his head. "Of course she couldn't do that. She was raised Catholic." Pain tightened the lines of his face. "And she didn't dare tell her father. So she stayed in New York. She went through the pregnancy alone, and had the baby by herself."

He turned and paced along the length of the terrace. His broad shoulders pulled the cloth of his shirt taut. "She died giving birth, just as her own mother had done eighteen years earlier."

"Oh, no." Susannah felt tears spring to her eyes.

"She died alone, afraid to seek help in a strange country where she had no true friends." The horror of the situation was written all over his face. "And because her *lover* had abandoned her."

He laid a fist on the terrace wall. Tension hardened every muscle in his body. "Someone, a neighbor, heard her…she must have been in terrible pain. They called an ambulance that was able to save the baby, but it was already too late for Marisa."

His chest rose and fell beneath his shirt. Fresh tears glittered in his eyes. "They found her address in Argentina somewhere in her possessions and called Ignacio to the hospital to claim the baby." He stared at her. "They'd already called Tarrant Hardcastle and he disavowed all responsibility."

"That's terrible." Susannah could barely manage to get out the words. They were so inadequate to the horror of the situation. It was hard to imagine even Tarrant Hardcastle being cold and cruel enough to abandon a tiny, helpless, motherless baby.

It dawned on her like a clap of thunder that Amado was that baby.

Hot tears rolled over her cheeks.

Amado frowned. "Why are you crying? Surely you knew all this."

"I didn't know anything." The words came out on a whine. "I'm so, so sorry. I can't believe that Tarrant…" A sob cracked her voice.

"My *real father*." He blew out a snort of disgust. "I curse the ground he walks on."

"I don't blame you." Susannah bit her lip. How on earth could she convince Amado to come back to New York with her now? She didn't even want to.

He inhaled deeply. "So Ignacio brought me back to Tierra de Oro. He didn't want me to suffer the shame of illegitimacy so he quickly married his longtime housekeeper, Clara. They told people Marisa had died in a car accident."

"I see." That explained how Clara came into the picture. "I'd think people would put two and two together, what with Marisa suddenly disappearing and a new baby arriving."

"My father said they pretended to have married earlier, but kept it secret because of the scandal of him marrying a servant." He snorted. "Substituting a petty piece of gossip for a real one."

He shook his head, looking out at the mountains. "Who knows, maybe everyone around here has known for years. But I didn't." He tapped his fist to his chest. "Thirty years on this earth and it never crossed my mind that I was anyone but the son of Clara and Ignacio Alvarez."

"Your father, I mean, Ignacio, told you all this?" If it was awkward for her to figure out what to call him, she could barely imagine how Amado must feel.

"Yes. And I got angry. Very angry." He fixed his gaze on the horizon. "How could he lie to me for so long?" The question rang with his pain and confusion.

Susannah wished she could think of something to say but her brain still buzzed with amazement at the strange situation.

He blew out a long breath. "And now he's ridden off into the hills and Clara is inconsolable."

Susannah was sweating inside her thin dress. "I'm so sorry. I don't know what to say."

Amado turned to her with a fierce expression. "Why should you be sorry? You're just doing your job." Anger curled in his voice, but once he looked at her, his gaze softened.

Her own distress must have been written all over her face. "You had no choice. With a jerk like that for a boss, you'd be fired if you didn't jump when he snapped his fingers."

Susannah exhaled. "You're right. I did it to keep my job. Now I'm wishing I hadn't."

He turned his profile to her and stared out at the mountains. Sun glittered off the icy peaks. "It's better the truth is out."

"Better? How is it better? Your family is in chaos." She glanced behind her, to where muffled sobs could still be heard through the door into the living room.

"Secrets are like poison in the system. They can hide for some time, but sooner or later, they'll weaken and destroy it." He turned to her, eyes narrowed. "Better to flush them out and face the consequences."

Despite his brave words, she could see the strain in every line of his body from the hard jut of his chin to the aggressive stance of his feet. He stood like someone trying to keep his balance in a world that had been upended.

"It's a different era now. There's no shame in being illegitimate."

"Doesn't bother me. I'm still the same person." His voice remained steady but a muscle tightened in his neck.

Was he? How could you be the same person after learning that the people you were closest to had lied to you throughout your whole life?

"You should come to New York. I know you've spoken to your sister Fiona on the phone…" She cringed, wondering exactly how Fiona had botched the phone call. Tarrant's spoiled daughter was so used to having everything her way, she didn't function all that well in the real world. Susannah couldn't help but feel sorry for her. How could you grow up to be a normal person with Tarrant Hardcastle as your role model? "You have a brother too. Dominic was abandoned, like you, but they found him and he's part of the family now."

Amado stared at her, as if the thought was sinking in. "A brother." He looked past her, out to the mountains.

Susannah swallowed. "There might be many of you. So far, Dominic's the only other one they've tracked down. He was raised by his mother. He's a year or so older than you."

His eyes locked onto hers. "I'd like to meet him."

"You'd like him. I work closely with him choosing wine for the restaurants."

"He works for Hardcastle Enterprises?" He looked appalled.

"Yes. He owns his own chain of food stores, too, but Tarrant convinced him to take over leadership of the company. It took some persuading to hear Dominic tell it. His attitude was similar to yours, but I guess Tarrant won him over in the end."

Amado's face hardened. "I have no interest in meeting the man who left my mother to die." Then, he inhaled, thoughtful. "But I do want to meet my brother and sister."

"They'd like to meet you, too." She hadn't seen Dominic and Fiona since the results. How could she look them in the eye when she'd slept with their brother?

What on earth had she been thinking?

She swallowed hard.

The sun glinted off Amado's proud profile. His sleeves were rolled up to reveal his tanned and muscled forearms. He was gorgeous.

Still, that was no excuse. Her behavior was beyond unprofessional. She'd have to do her best to stay far away from him while he was in New York. Then he'd go back to Argentina and no one would be the wiser.

"Why are you backing away from me?" He glanced down at her feet.

She froze, unaware that her body had been putting a safe distance between them. "I'm not."

"Yes, you are." He tilted his head. Humor glinted in the coffee-brown depths of his eyes. "Little did I know what I was getting into when I invited you in for wine and *alfajores*. I thought my parents were so rude to try to get rid of you. Now, I see, they wanted to protect me. To protect us all."

He took a step toward her. Desire throbbed in her veins as her body responded to the raw aggression of his gesture.

"Don't think you can walk away now."

Susannah stood rigid on the veranda of his house, her slim body shivering with tension.

In spite of everything, Amado wanted to take her in his arms.

Her prim carriage and her clipped, businesslike speech were only one side of Susannah Clarke. He'd enjoyed the delicious privilege of seeing the other side.

He hadn't stopped thinking about her since she left. About her serious and thoughtful expressions. About the arch of her body under his. The way she had clung to him, her limbs taut with arousal. How she'd writhed beneath him as their passion built to exquisite agony, followed by an explosive exhale of sweet relief.

It was a night he'd never forget, with a woman he couldn't get out of his mind.

Especially now that she'd turned his life upside down.

Her elegant chin tilted as she defied his challenge. He took another step forward. Uninvited, he slid his hand under her jacket and ran his palm over her breast.

She gasped. Her nipple tightened under his palm. And she didn't step back.

Desire spiked through him as he cupped her breast. Peered into her mysterious dark eyes. Her mouth closed, then opened again. A silent protest? Her lips were naturally dark, the color of smashed berries, and he longed to crush his mouth over them and drink deep.

One more step brought his chest within inches of hers. His hand still on her breast, testing, teasing, he inhaled the scent of her in the hot afternoon air.

He could already taste her desire on his tongue, smell it on the wind. Also her fear.

He slid his hands around her back, pulling her close. She stood like a statue, the air between them thick with tension.

He laid his palms over the dip of her waist, enjoyed the curve of her backside. He could hear her breathing, feel her arousal swelling like a bud thickening and preparing to open.

Against her will.

If he lifted her dress he'd bet her panties were already damp with longing. His erection strained against his zipper.

Maybe he'd take her here, on the hard stone of the patio, under the unforgiving sun. With the mountains watching in stern silence.

Her lips parted and a shaky breath escaped. Her eyes slid closed for a second as her insides quivered under his fingers. He felt her muscles contract under her neat dress.

Waiting for him.

Hoping.

Their tongues clashed as he kissed her, hot and hard. The taste of her was intoxicating, a drug he'd craved.

Her body crushed against his, lithe with passion as she kissed him back, clutching his face to hers with eager hands.

A low, guttural moan escaped her as he lifted her dress and tested her slick heat with his fingers.

He slid a finger into her silky depths and she rocked against him. He held her steady with one hand behind her back as he brought her swiftly to climax with his finger and thumb.

His power over her was absolute at this moment. Eyes closed, she gave herself over to the fierce magic of the moment.

The tremor raged through her and he caught her as she almost lost her footing. Panting, she rested against him for a second.

Then she realized he'd stopped and was just standing there.

Staring at her.

Prim and proper Susannah Clarke's eyes were black with passion. A dark flush heightened her proud cheekbones and her long dark hair hung about her shoulders, wild from his caresses.

He let her dress fall back to her calves.

Didn't say a word.

Her glaze of passion lessened and confusion flickered in her eyes.

Good.

She smoothed the front of her dress, suddenly self-conscious. He could see her nipples, still peaked under the soft fabric.

"You don't find it easy to say no to me, do you?"

His cruel question made her blink.

Why should he be the one lying awake, tormented by memories of that night? Let her suffer. So cool and calm and collected, as she delivered her life-shattering news.

She checked the buttons on the front of her dress.

"Don't worry, you still look virginal."

His mocking tone made her blink again.

"Though, of course, we both know better." He tilted his

head. Contemplated the possibility of touching her firm breasts again. "What would your big boss say, if he knew?"

Her eyes widened. "You wouldn't?"

"How do you know? I'm a virtual stranger. We spent one day together." He licked his lips. "And one night."

She backed away. This time he let her.

"You know me as Amado Alvarez, of Tierra de Oro." He snorted. "Or at least that's who I used to be until you showed up." He hesitated. Watching her squirm. "He would have kept your sexy secrets. Amado Alvarez was a man of honor."

He inhaled, then let out a long, slow exhale. "But apparently, I'm not the man I thought I was. I'm the son of this...*Tarrant Hardcastle*." He spat the name like a bad taste. "Who knows what I'm truly capable of?"

The patio doors flung open and Ignacio crashed out onto the terrace. "What the hell is she doing back here?" he raged, eyes bulging.

Amado froze. He'd never seen his father like this. Ignacio could express strong feelings in an argument, or when his favorite football team was losing, but Amado'd never seen him yell at a woman.

Since Susannah showed up, bringing the ugly truth about his parentage, everything had changed. He didn't know who he or anyone else was anymore.

Susannah shrank away, tugging her jacket over her dress as if covering her nakedness.

Ignacio moved toward her. "Get out, now! I've never laid a hand on a woman, but by God, I'll throw you out myself if you don't—"

"Calm yourself." Amado stepped forward and grabbed his father's arm. "Susannah is here on *business*." He shot her a dark look.

She made a vain attempt to tuck her gorgeous wild hair behind her shoulders.

"She has no business here but to disrupt our lives."

Susannah stepped back. Amado couldn't resist a powerful urge to defend her. "She brought the truth, didn't she?"

His father frowned.

"The truth that you planned to keep from me. Don't I have a right to know the circumstances of my own birth? To know who brought me into this world?"

The force in his own voice surprised him. But suddenly he did feel strongly about it.

"It was for the best." His father rubbed his temples. "I thought it was for the best."

Anger heated Amado's blood as long-buried resentments rose to the surface. Nagging doubts he'd silenced for years now crept out of the darkness. He was beginning to suspect he had every reason to despise Ignacio for his lies. "Is that why you drove away Valentina?"

He still remembered the heated shouting matches he'd had with his father when he was nineteen and desperately in love. Ignacio had point-blank forbidden the marriage, saying she was unsuitable as an Alvarez bride.

He'd wondered at the time if Ignacio was secretly behind her sudden change of heart. Now Amado saw the ugly truth unfold in front of his eyes. "You wouldn't accept her as my wife, not because *she* was illegitimate, but because you didn't want anyone to find out that I am, too?"

Ignacio hesitated. Rubbed a hand over his face. "If you'd married as a minor, they would have seen your birth certificate."

The confession chilled his blood. He'd suspected the truth all along, but never been sure. Her change of heart had been too sudden, too final.

Now, he knew. The man who called himself his own father had driven away the woman he loved. "You chose your lie over my life."

Amado shoved a hand through his hair. The injustice burned him. Years of lies that had warped his existence. His comfortable life here at Tierra de Oro came at a harsh cost, especially to the two woman who should have been closest to him.

"All this time, Marisa has been a silent shadow. She was the sister I never knew and who I knew *nothing* about. It's not right. She was a real person."

He realized his fist was clenched, but he couldn't seem to unlock it. "She was my mother and you shouldn't have swept her story out the door with yesterday's dust." His voice trembled with rage.

"She died so young." His father shook his head. Amado resisted the urge to step forward and put a hand on his shoulder. "She never had a chance to become a woman."

"She *was* a woman. You may not have wanted to accept it, but your little girl grew up. She bore a child."

"I don't...I don't..." his father spluttered.

"You don't want to think about that." Amado's words shattered the stunned quiet. "You never did. You just wanted her to be your little girl forever, which is probably why she ran away to New York in the first place. You can't keep everything the same as it was in the nineteenth century. Like the estate, we must change and grow in order to keep living."

"If only she'd never met that Tarrant Hardcastle." The words dripped from his father's tongue like acid.

"But she did. And now I must meet him, too." The resolve formed in Amado's mind as he said the words. This family was done with ignoring unpleasant realities. He wanted to face them head on.

For years, he'd tried to forget the pain of losing his fiancée. He'd always suspected that Ignacio had had a hand in Valentina's leaving, but to hear him admit it—

Adrenaline flashed through his muscles and he struggled to keep himself under control.

He was done being played. Perhaps meeting his birth father would bring some reality back into this charade.

"I'll meet Tarrant Hardcastle and make up my own mind about him."

"He's not your father. He didn't raise you."

"He bears half the responsibility for bringing me into this world, whether he wanted to or not." He drew in a breath as anger heated his blood. "Now he thinks he can fold me to his bosom like a long-lost sheep?" He blew out a hard breath. "We'll see. For now, I want to look into the face of the man who left my mother to die."

He glanced at Susannah, who'd watched their exchange, her kiss-reddened lips parted in stunned silence.

He cursed the strong feelings Susannah herself had awakened in him. He couldn't seem to get her out of his mind. Her solemn gaze haunted him, and her hungry passion.

And he had to admit that, along with the chaos she'd unleashed, came the fresh air of truth.

He drew in a deep breath and stared at her. "I'll come to New York with you."

Six

Susannah and Amado stood side by side in the elevator, ascending to Tarrant's private office on an upper floor of his Fifth Avenue retail palace. Amado's tailored suit gave him a formal, distant air. Usually unruly and windblown, his dark hair was slicked back to reveal his strong features.

He didn't speak. He seemed lost in thought—and who wouldn't be?

Tarrant, his wife Samantha, daughter Fiona and new-found son Dominic were waiting for them.

Susannah was only there because Amado wouldn't let her go.

He'd insisted that she spend the night with him in his room at The Pierre. There he drew her into the tight circle the two of them made, away from prying eyes. He worked his dark, sensual magic on her, turning her inside and out in a realm of intense pleasure.

She didn't even try to resist.

He needed her. Longing and tension snapped in the air. She could taste his anger in the heat of his skin. Smell his hunger in his musky male scent.

His lovemaking was aggressive, demanding, unbearably erotic.

Afterward, they'd lain tangled in the expensive sheets, exhausted and more wound-up than ever.

Ding.

The elevator stopped. Amado hooked his arm around her elbow as if to foil any attempted escape.

She tried to pull her arm back. "What if they think we're…?" Panic rippled through her.

"What if they do?" His voice had an edge to it that she hadn't heard before. He didn't look at her.

"But this is my job," she rasped.

"And you do it so well." He raised an eyebrow before coolly withdrawing his arm from hers.

A chill descended as her arm fell to her side.

He thought she'd slept with him to get the job done?

Had she?

"Amado!" A slender blonde raced into the reception area. She clapped her hands to her mouth at the sight of him, apparently overwhelmed by emotion.

Amado stopped.

Susannah realized introductions were up to her. "Amado, this is Samantha Hardcastle, she's your…your father's wife."

His third wife, to be precise.

Amado held out his hand and shook Samantha's. He murmured a polite greeting in his accented English.

Susannah could see he was surprised by how young Samantha was. Maybe even younger than him.

Susannah thought that, underneath her polished society-wife exterior, Samantha Hardcastle was one of the nicest and most genuine people she'd ever met. Still, she refrained from pointing out to Amado that she was now officially his stepmom.

"Tarrant wanted to come out and meet you himself but he's weak today. I'm sure Susannah told you that he's ill." Samantha's eyes shone with emotion. "Please come in. We're all so happy you're here."

Amado's expression was unreadable.

Susannah tensed with anticipation. *Please let it go well. Let Amado find some happiness in this family drama she'd laid at his door.*

She hung back as Samantha led Amado into Tarrant's spacious office. Dazzling afternoon light streamed through the tall windows that looked down over Central Park.

Dominic, the first unclaimed son of Tarrant's to be located, stepped forward. He ushered Amado into the hushed space, shook his hand formally, then—as if on instinct—pulled him into a deep embrace.

Dominic had been chosen to replace Tarrant as President after Tarrant's death, despite a publicized scandal about his affair with a corporate spy at Hardcastle Enterprises.

Bella Soros, the scientist and mole he'd uncovered both literally and figuratively, was now his wife and a key figure at Hardcastle. Susannah spotted her standing to one side, watching her husband's newfound brother with her perceptive gray gaze.

Emotion crackled in the air as Amado bent to greet the sickly tycoon, who could barely rise from his chair. Tarrant clasped Amado's hand in both of his, "My son, I'm so glad we found you."

Susannah found herself getting choked up. Perhaps because Tarrant seemed so frail—so old, even though he was only sixty-seven. He looked like a man with a short time left to live and she prayed that Amado would be gentle with him.

To err is human. Forgiveness is divine. The familiar words from her childhood rang in her mind.

Would she be able to forgive a sin of the magnitude of Tarrant's?

Tarrant praised Amado's wines in appreciative detail, which brought Amado out and engaged him in conversation. He stood tall and dignified, polite and reserved, as Tarrant introduced him to his daughter Fiona.

The only child actually born to Tarrant within the confines of a legal marriage, Fiona was the daughter of his second wife. Susannah thought her somewhat spoiled and flighty, no doubt a result of her indulgent surroundings. She worked at Hardcastle Enterprises but seemed to drift from one department to the next, without settling into a real career.

Fiona was tight-lipped, barely verbal, her abundant red hair pulled back into a tight chignon. Amado shook her hand, then leaned forward to kiss her on the cheek, which caused a flicker of emotion in her green eyes.

It must be hard to be Tarrant's only child for so long, then have the limelight stolen by the tall, handsome men Tarrant now claimed as his sons and heirs.

Amado, proud and restrained, murmured that he'd like to speak to Tarrant Hardcastle—he called him by his full name—alone. Susannah hurried from the room, heart pounding, and slipped away to her office.

The door closed behind his newfound brother and sister, leaving Amado alone with his father.

His father.

The man who sowed the seed that would become him, then abandoned the garden.

"You're angry."

Tarrant's words startled him.

"Yes, I am." He looked down at the thin, suntanned face, with its high cheekbones and piercing blue-green eyes. The man who'd left his mother to die.

"I didn't know about you." Amado studied Tarrant's face as he spoke. "Ignacio Alvarez raised me as his son, and his wife claimed to be my mother."

"You were lucky to be raised by such caring people."

Tarrant's platitude heated Amado's blood. "Lucky indeed. After being abandoned by the man who gave life to me."

"I know apologies are inadequate. There's no excuse for what I did. I was young and stupid."

Tarrant's chest heaved inside his crisp blue shirt. "I knew your mother was pregnant. I told her to take care of it, that I'd reimburse her, but she wouldn't hear of it. I told her that if she didn't, she'd see no more of me."

Tarrant paused and frowned. "I never saw her alive again." He looked up at Amado, eyes shining with unshed tears. "She chose you over me. And a very wise choice it was."

Amado's heart seized at the honest confession. Then his muscles tightened. "I wish I had known her myself."

"It's my great sorrow that you never will." Tarrant pushed long, tanned fingers through his thick silver hair. "She was a beautiful, lively woman. A talented painter with a big future ahead of her. I couldn't understand why she wanted to throw that away to take care of a child."

"She faced up to her responsibility." Amado spoke through gritted teeth.

"Something I could never bring myself to do. I don't ask

you to forgive me, because I know you won't. You can't. I only hope that you will consider yourself a part of our family."

Tarrant took a drink from a glass filled with clear liquid. "It means so much to my wife to bring you together with Dominic and Fiona. I think she's afraid the Hardcastle family will disintegrate after I die. She never had children of her own and she sees you all as her family."

Amado blinked. Tarrant's wife? The stylish blonde who looked all of twenty-five? She'd be a merry widow laughing all the way to the bank.

"Is this why you brought me here? To make your wife happy?"

Had his life been turned upside down to provide entertainment for his father's bored trophy wife? His blood surged near its boiling point.

Tarrant rose from his chair. It took considerable effort, from the pained expression on his face. Amado found himself reaching forward to offer a helping hand under his elbow. "No. I wanted you here. For me. The selfish wish of a dying man to meet his son."

Amado swallowed. The emotion plain in Tarrant's face tugged at his heart.

"I'm so proud of what you've accomplished. Susannah brought me your wines and told me you've been developing the vineyards since you were a child. You deserve all the success you've worked hard for and so much more. And I hope that we at Hardcastle Enterprises can help you expand your business to the next level."

Amado gripped Tarrant's bony elbow, partly to prevent the unsteady man from falling back into his chair, and partly because he didn't want to let go.

Foreign emotions jolted through him. In spite of everything, he felt a sudden deep bond with the man before him.

It must have taken courage to face up to his failure as a father and invite censure and anger into his life in the form of a neglected child.

Not quite sure what he was doing, Amado pulled Tarrant into his arms and hugged him tightly. He couldn't stop himself. "You didn't know my mother would die," he heard himself whisper. "No one could have known that." Pain throbbed inside him. It had always hurt him that he'd never met his sister. Now that he knew she was his mother, the loss felt fresh and raw.

Tarrant inhaled. "She would have been so proud of you. She used to talk about your estate—Tierra de Oro, isn't it?—as if it was some kind of magical Eden. I know she'd be so happy that you are living there and taking care of it for the next generation."

Amado swallowed hard, trying to choke back the fierce emotion flooding through him.

He knew so little about Marisa. Ignacio and Clara became agitated and shared pained glances if he even mentioned her name. He'd always assumed they were so torn up by her premature death—in an "accident"—that they couldn't bear to talk about her.

He knew Marisa's mother had also died young, and that his father had been single for almost twenty years before marrying again. The aging newlyweds had borne only one child.

At least, that's what he'd been told.

He realized he was still holding Tarrant tight, and he pulled back. Drew in a deep breath.

He was sad for the dying man who wouldn't live to see his own grandchildren.

But forgiveness?

Not really.

The door opened and Samantha put her head around it. She smiled. He wondered if she'd been listening at the door.

"Amado, Dominic and Fiona want to take you out to dinner. Show you the city. Please say you will."

Big blue eyes implored him.

"I'd be delighted." He managed to keep his voice calm and polite. Nodded to Tarrant.

"We'll talk more later." The tycoon seemed to have regained his arrogant demeanor. "We'll do some business." A satisfied smile spread across his tanned face and good humor twinkled in his aqua eyes. "I want to help you bring your wines to the States."

"I'd like that."

Why not? Perhaps something positive could come out of this mess.

Where was Susannah? Had she snuck off and abandoned him now that her work was done?

Inevitable desire crept over him at the thought of her. Of her dark, lush mouth. Her haunting gaze.

Her thoughtful silences.

If she thought she could bring him here and throw him at his father's feet like a lamb to slaughter, then disappear out of his life, she was very much mistaken.

"I'd like Susannah to return to Tierra de Oro. To develop a business plan." He tilted his head, waiting for Tarrant's reaction.

The older man's eyes narrowed. He could hear cogs turning in that sharp mind.

Did he know there was more between them than professional cordiality? A man like Tarrant Hardcastle, ruled by fleeting passions and expensive indulgences, probably encouraged his staff to accomplish their goals by any means necessary.

Perhaps she would receive a bonus for her little coup.

"Of course. I'll instruct her to stay as long as you wish."
Tarrant gave him a knowing glance.

Amado recoiled inwardly, as if Tarrant had said, "I'll
have her scrubbed and sent to your tent."

But isn't that what he wanted?

"Susannah! Oh, thank goodness you're there."

Susannah, roused from a deep sleep, tried to figure out
the owner of the voice blasting out of her phone.

"We're taking Amado to a *milonga,* to make him feel
at home. You *must* come."

Fiona.

Susannah's heart sank. Could she say no to Daddy's
Little Princess?

"Gosh, I'm very tired. I haven't had a decent night's
sleep in…" She was too tired to remember when she'd had
a decent night's sleep.

Certainly not last night, in Amado's hotel room. And the
two previous nights had been spent on long-haul flights to
and from Santiago, Chile. The latter, locked in intellectual
combat with Amado on a variety of challenging topics including the usually off-limits religion and politics.

She sagged against the cool white sheets in her Spar-
tan apartment.

"You have two hours to take a nap, then meet us in the
lobby. We'll all take a car downtown together."

The dial tone brooked no contradiction.

Susannah fumbled with her alarm clock, hoping that it
would ring loud enough to wake her from whatever fitful
slumber she could claim in two hours.

Amado must have asked for her to come. Was he trying
to kill her?

Maybe this was his way of getting revenge on her for shaking him out of his comfortable ignorance.

And what the heck was a *milonga?*

Susannah leaped off the bus and darted along Fifth Avenue, already five minutes late. The icy December blast was a harsh contrast to the Southern Hemisphere warmth she'd left behind in Mendoza. She clutched her wool coat around her skimpy black wrap dress as she clattered along the cement sidewalk.

With any luck they'd have left without her.

But no. The imposing Fiona stood on the sidewalk in front of the Hardcastle building, clad in a fitted leather jacket, her green dress whipping against her long, elegant legs. "Finally!"

Amado leaned against a wall of the building, devastatingly elegant in a dark suit. He must be freezing out here in the cold. He didn't move when he saw her, but she felt his gaze sizzle through her like a heat wave.

"I'm sorry, there was way more traffic than I expected."

"Never mind that. Get in." Fiona gestured to the waiting stretch limo.

Susannah folded herself into the darkest corner. Dominic and Bella flirted with each other on one of the long, bench seats. Amado flashed a wicked glance at her as he entered, then he sat next to Fiona and proceeded to lavish her with his masculine charm.

Susannah stared hard at her clutch purse.

Fiona leaned forward. "Amado, you're going to love this place. It's really intimate, started by a couple from Buenos Aires who teach tango classes."

She touched his knee. Her long, pale fingers rested for a moment on his powerful thighs.

A surge of irritation pushed Susannah forward. "Amado's from the country. Mendoza isn't anywhere near Buenos Aires."

Amado's black gaze rested on her face. "You think I don't know how to tango?"

Susannah pressed herself back into her corner, shrinking from his forceful presence. She shrugged, not wanting to accuse the reputedly dramatic Fiona of making assumptions.

"Do you?" Fiona leaned into him, her gold hoop earrings swinging.

"I guess you'll have to find out." He smiled warmly at Fiona. Susannah cursed the ugly possessive attitude that made her resent Fiona's instant intimacy with Amado.

Fiona had every right to be intimate with him. She was his sister. Susannah, on the contrary, did not. Once he went back to Argentina, she'd see him maybe once a year at tasting time.

Perhaps not even then.

Still, it had only been a few hours since he'd trailed his fingers over her bare skin and licked her to a shuddering climax in his hotel bed.

She tried to keep her breathing steady. *Focus on the lights of the city flashing past outside the tinted window.*

Amado lingered in the limo until all the others climbed out, then offered his arm to Susannah. "I'm glad you came."

Anticipation shivered through her as she took his arm. The fine fabric of his dark suit tickled her fingertips and made all her tiny, invisible hairs stand on end.

She wasn't even sure where they were. Somewhere downtown. A dark awning shaded the door of the club from the streetlights. A line of hip and elegant patrons waited outside on the cold sidewalk, but Fiona marched right up to the door and whispered something to the scary-looking bouncer.

He ushered them in. She could feel Amado's strong arm through the sleeve of his suit. As they stepped through the door, the music beckoned to them, rhythmic and seductive.

Lucky thing *she* didn't know how to tango. At least she had a good excuse for not making a fool of herself.

They descended some stairs, and emerged into a loft-like space. Tables clothed in linen ringed a dance floor, already packed with writhing bodies.

A live band with a row of accordionists crammed onto the small stage, energizing the room with the urgent throb of the tango.

They gathered at a table and ordered drinks. Fiona chattered excitedly about the tango lessons she'd been taking and wasn't it a fantastic coincidence that her new brother was from Argentina?

Susannah sipped her drink while Fiona pulled Amado, laughing, from his seat and onto the dance floor.

Dominic and Bella followed suit. They both claimed to have never tangoed before, but Susannah found herself transfixed by the passion that flashed between them like oxygen fanning a fire. The tall and striking Dominic radiated controlled intensity while Bella, a research chemist with the body of a 1950s sex goddess, flowed around him like molten metal.

She snuck a glance at Amado and Fiona. Her blood pressure spiked at the sight of his hands splayed over her bare spine. She knew the touch of those fingers, forceful yet tender, and her body ached for it.

Susannah! He's not yours. Be happy for him that he's

found a family he didn't know about. Maybe, if she hadn't played his sensual games, she'd never have persuaded him to part with the DNA that was the first step on his journey here.

Fiona flicked her legs around his, twirling in a practiced and elegant motion.

Susannah snatched her gaze away. The ugly green beast of jealously was so unfamiliar she had no idea how to handle it.

How could she begrudge him a dance with his own sister, for crying out loud? What kind of selfish, egotistical maniac was she?

She glanced up again, over the rim of her vanilla martini, and this time her eyes met Amado's. Longing flashed through her. As he spun Fiona in an elegant turn, he kept his focus on Susannah, depriving her of breath.

He's playing with you.

Was this why he'd brought her here tonight? To tempt her and toy with her, as sweet revenge for the way she'd upended his life?

The song ended suddenly, and Susannah found herself fidgeting and glancing every which way, to avoid the sight of the flushed and excited dancers returning to the table.

Dominic gave his wife a sensual kiss. Amado eased Fiona back into her chair.

Then he walked over to her.

"Your turn."

"I don't know how to tango."

"No matter." He held out his hand.

"Seriously, I'll look like a fool."

"If you dance, you might look like a fool. If you sit there in your chair and miss all the fun, everyone will *know* you're a fool." His eyes glittered a challenge.

She rose to her feet, damned if she did and damned if she didn't. Amado hooked his arm around her waist, and practically carried her onto the small dance floor. Already at least fifteen other couples swirled to the music.

"But I…"

Amado silenced her with a finger to her lips. "Don't think. Just listen to the music." He leaned in close, his breath hot on her ear. "Listen to your body. Dance with *me*."

Her belly tightened in response to the sensual rasp of his voice. She drew in a shaky breath.

Her black wrap dress had a long slit down the back of the bodice, and he slid his fingers inside it. Her eyes widened. Surely he didn't want the others to know they were intimate?

He pulled her close until her body was almost crushed against his.

Almost.

A scant half-inch of superheated space separated their hips. He inclined his head until his cheek was almost touching hers and she could anticipate the slight roughness of his skin.

He took her other hand and held it lightly in his, then he stepped forward, into her.

Instinctively she stepped back, and he turned, whirling them half around. Then he stepped back. His hand on her waist pulled her with him, and she placed her toes between his. Forward and back, around, his hands and the movements of his feet guided her through the throng of dancers.

The music, taut and rhythmic, strung the air with tension. It thrummed in her body as time and again she stepped into Amado's embrace, anticipating his body heat. Then he pulled away, leaving a tiny ache.

The Silhouette Reader Service — Here's how it works:

Accepting your 2 free books and 2 free mystery gifts places you under no obligation to buy anything. You may keep the books and gifts and return the shipping statement marked "cancel". If you do not cancel, about a month later we'll send you 6 additional books and bill you just $4.05 each in the U.S. or $4.74 each in Canada. That is a savings of at least 15% off the cover price. It's quite a bargain! Shipping and handling is just 25¢ per book. You may cancel at any time, but if you choose to continue, every month we'll send you 6 more books, which you may either purchase at the discount price or return to us and cancel your subscription.

Terms and prices subject to change without notice. Prices do not include applicable taxes. Sales tax applicable in N.Y. Canadian residents will be charged applicable provincial taxes and GST. Offer not valid in Quebec. All orders subject to approval. Credit or debit balances in a customer's account(s) may be offset by any other outstanding balance owed by or to the customer. Please allow 4 to 6 weeks for delivery. Offer available while quantities last.

www.ReaderService.com

NO POSTAGE
NECESSARY
IF MAILED
IN THE
UNITED STATES

BUSINESS REPLY MAIL
FIRST-CLASS MAIL   PERMIT NO. 717   BUFFALO, NY

POSTAGE WILL BE PAID BY ADDRESSEE

SILHOUETTE READER SERVICE
PO BOX 1867
BUFFALO NY 14240-9952

Do You Have the LUCKY KEY?

PLAY THE *Lucky Key Game*

and you can get

Scratch the gold areas with a coin. Then check below to see the books and gifts you can get!

FREE BOOKS and FREE GIFTS!

YES! I have scratched off the gold areas. Please send me the 2 FREE BOOKS and 2 FREE GIFTS, worth about $10, for which I qualify. I understand I am under no obligation to purchase any books, as explained on the back of this card.

DETACH AND MAIL CARD TODAY!

(S-D-03/09)

326 SDL EXE2   225 SDL EW6E

FIRST NAME	LAST NAME

ADDRESS

APT.#	CITY

www.ReaderService.com

STATE/PROV.   ZIP/POSTAL CODE

🔑🔑🔑🔑 2 free books plus 2 free gifts   🔑🔑🔑 1 free book

🔑🔑🔑 2 free books   🔑🔑 Try Again!

He drew her with him, leading her on a sensual journey that never quite reached its end.

Occasionally, he did one wicked move where he stepped between her legs, parting them, overtly sexual.

Then he would step back and draw her into an elegant turn, as if nothing had happened.

Energy snapped between them, stinging her skin with adrenaline and tightening her nipples inside her thin dress.

I'm dancing. Astonishment rippled through her as they moved across the floor, weaving through the elegant *tangueros* like they did this every night.

It felt as complicated, as astonishing, as natural as...

Sex.

The song ended. Susannah's heart pounded as Amado lifted her hand and kissed it.

The perfect gentleman.

He led her back to the table without a word, giving her nothing but the sight of his arrogant profile.

Susannah sank into her chair, aching with freshly inflamed desire. Amado sipped his drink and gracefully accepted Fiona's gushing compliments. He laughed and said that no, he'd never taken lessons. His first girlfriend—older than he—had taught him everything he needed to know.

Susannah was jealous of her, too.

She laughed off Fiona's tight-lipped compliments, giving full credit to Amado.

Apparently he could make her do anything. In his hands, she turned into someone else. Someone wilder, more natural, more alive.

If she hadn't met him, she'd probably never have found out that she was capable of heights of embarrassing ecstasy in the bedroom. Of an exquisite, lust-laden tango in a crowded room.

And she still wasn't sure if it was a good or bad thing that she did know.

She survived two more breath-stealing, blood-heating dances with him. Then he kissed her good-night, a chaste lip on her cheek, and said goodbye.

She went home alone, her body throbbing and aching with unspent desire.

No problem. He'd kept their secret. She'd keep her job.

Get back to her normal life. That was what she wanted, wasn't it?

Seven

He'd been gone three days. No goodbye, no warning, just gone.

Susannah was curled up in the armchair in her apartment. On the sofa, her best friend Suki sat with her arms wrapped around her long legs. "Sweetheart, you look…haunted."

"Oh, nonsense." Susannah leaped to her feet and swept into her tiny kitchen to put on the kettle.

"It's that wine grower, isn't it?"

"They're called vintners."

"Hah. See? You're not even denying it."

"Chamomile or lemon ginger?"

"What rakish choices. I see you've sworn off caffeine. Aren't you worried the ginger will be too stimulating?" She winked.

Susannah crossed her hands over her chest and glared at Suki. "What kind of friend are you?"

"The annoying kind who won't let you tell me everything's fine when it obviously isn't. Ever since you went to Argentina, you've been acting strange. Your cheeks are hollow and your eyes have a strange gleam to them."

"Maybe I picked up a fever on my travels."

"There's no doubt about that. I'm just trying to learn a little more about the man who gave it to you. Is he *devastatingly* handsome?"

Susannah walked across the room and collapsed on the sofa next to her friend with a sigh. "Yes. I'm afraid he is."

"Oh, no. They're the worst." Suki winced.

Tall, blond, blue-eyed, with perfectly chiseled features and a rosy complexion, Suki had the kind of beauty that made heads swivel when she entered a room. Her stunning looks also attracted the worst cads and users known to mankind. Her romantic advice to the far-less-experienced Susannah usually consisted of heartfelt cautions.

"Did you sleep with him already, or did he turn you into a zombie with just a kiss?"

"I slept with him." Susannah stared at the wood floor. "It seemed like an okay idea. A fun vacation fling. You know, the kind everyone has." She glanced up.

"You're not everyone." Suki clucked her tongue. "Don't say I didn't warn you."

"You warned me Argentine men think they're God's gift to women."

"Apparently you've had the misfortune to find one who actually is. At least, if that feverish glitter in your eye is anything to go by."

Susannah bit her lip. "He's an amazing lover."

"That's not everything, you know. He probably can't string two thoughts together if they're not about wine."

Susannah sighed. "I wish. I shared an overnight flight

with him and he has interesting opinions about all sorts of things. He's a real thinker."

"Just like you." Suki narrowed her eyes.

"He's not like me. As I said, he's gorgeous. He probably has women falling all over him every week. He certainly knows how to drive a woman wild. He gave me a foot massage that made me putty in his hands."

Suki's eyes widened. "People into feet are kinky."

Susannah frowned. "It didn't feel kinky at all. It felt…generous. He seemed to genuinely enjoy taking care of me. Making me feel *at home*. He used that phrase a lot."

"Oh, boy. He does sound dangerous." Suki looked fascinated. "And he's your boss's son?"

"Biological son, yes." She blew out a breath. "I really didn't think he would be, or I would never have—you know."

"That is a bit unfortunate, isn't it? Still, it'll mean he's loaded."

"Like I care about that? Besides, he's made a success of his own vineyard. He doesn't need Tarrant Hardcastle's money."

"Sweetheart, everyone needs Tarrant Hardcastle's money."

"I don't."

"Yes, you do. Otherwise, why are you working for him?"

"Ouch." The kettle started to whistle and Susannah jumped up to get it, glad of the distraction. "I took the job because I like to travel."

"You like to keep moving so you don't have to deal with anyone for more than a few days."

"Nonsense."

"Is it? Why do you like to travel so much? You've spent your whole life moving from place to place. I'd think you'd be dying to settle down for a change."

"Perhaps I just haven't found the right place to settle

yet." She poured the hot water over two chamomile tea bags. Nice and soothing.

An image of mountains crept into her consciousness. Snowcapped and silent, standing sentry over rows and rows of lush, tenderly cared for vines.

It's a special place.

Her own words came back to haunt her.

No wonder she looked haunted.

If Amado was a ghost, she could get him exorcised from her imagination. She wouldn't be tormented by the memory of his fingers on her skin, his lips at her throat. By the sensation of him moving deep inside her, slow and powerful…

"Helloooooo, did you hear a word I just said?"

"What?"

"Oh, dear. So when are you going back to visit him?"

"Never, as far as I know. He went back three days ago and didn't even call to say goodbye. The last time I saw him was when we tangoed together."

She stirred the tea, banging the spoon against the china. Tears threatened and she swallowed hard to shove them back down.

"A fun vacation fling with the boss's son." Suki shook her head. "I guess it might be better if you didn't see him again. Jobs like yours don't grow on trees. Or grape vines."

"I know," she managed. "I need to get a grip. I have a trip to South Africa to reschedule." She put the spoon on the counter. "And Tarrant wants to see me in his office tomorrow."

Suki raised a brow. "Uh-oh."

"Your mission is to draw Amado into the fold." Tarrant leaned forward and picked up a gold-plated pen from his neat mahogany desk.

Susannah felt a painful throb start somewhere at the base of her skull.

"I want concrete ties with his estate. I want him *excited* to do business with us. There will be a handsome bonus in it for you."

He scribbled something on a piece of paper, then handed it to her.

A check. For ten thousand dollars.

Her mouth fell open.

"I'm very pleased with the work you've done so far." Tarrant leaned back into his chair. "Delighted, in fact. You've gone above and beyond the call of duty."

Susannah froze. Had Amado told him she'd slept with him to get the DNA? He was angry with her and Tarrant and...everyone. Who knew how he might lash out?

"I know you've had to reschedule trips and reorganize your calendar to fly to Argentina twice at a moment's notice. Don't think I take that for granted."

Susannah realized that the hand holding the check had started to shake. She snatched it into her lap.

Tarrant looked much healthier than he had the previous week and his face beamed with uncomplicated cheer. She suspected he didn't know about the affair. If he did, he wouldn't order her to go back down there. Would he?

Her stomach churned. Did Amado even want to see her again?

He'd invited her to his Manhattan hotel room and driven her wild with pleasure, his passion almost angry in its intensity. On the tango expedition, he'd tormented her into a state of tortured arousal—only to peck her good-night on the cheek.

And that was that. She found out third-hand he'd returned to Argentina.

Without saying goodbye.

She shrank into her chair, the enormous check clutched in her sweating hand. Blood money, in a literal sense. She was paid for retrieving Amado's genetic material. For cornering him and bringing him back here.

And now she had to shove herself down his throat again?

Hey, guess what, I'm back!

She could always quit her job right now. Hand the check back and retain the last pathetic shreds of her dignity.

But then she would certainly never see Amado again.

Those final tatters fell silently to the carpet as she nodded. "I'll arrange a return trip for next week. Which wines were you hoping to secure for our cellars?"

"All of them."

Astride his horse, Amado watched from the hillside. The small white car approaching the house could be carrying only one person.

He knew because his skin prickled with awareness.

Susannah.

His horse pranced sideways and he lost sight of her as she entered the avenue of cypress.

No need to rush back. She'd be waiting for him when he arrived.

He'd instructed Rosa to put her in Marisa's old room. The whole house was suddenly haunted by the ghosts of the past. Surely it was only right that Susannah get more intimately acquainted with them?

Ignacio hadn't spoken to him since his trip to New York. Or was it he who hadn't spoken to Ignacio? Now that Ignacio's deception was revealed, Amado found himself questioning the man's authority over any aspect of his life.

Old wounds had broken open and festered in the sour air of mistrust.

And Susannah was to blame.

She'd reawakened feelings he hadn't experienced since Ignacio drove away the woman he loved more than ten years ago. Valentina taught him to dance and taught him to love. But she hadn't been a suitable wife for a son of Ignacio Alvarez.

Amado issued a curse that rang in the air. What a joke.

When she left, he tried to follow her but she'd turned him away. She'd implied that she didn't want him without the estate.

Proud and angry, he'd returned home, thrown himself into his work and moved on.

Now he wondered how much Ignacio's little misguided attempt to save the family honor had cost Valentina, as well as himself.

He hadn't lived as a monk in the years since. He enjoyed the company of women. Loved to cherish and pleasure them, savor a delicious tango between the sheets, then leave them with a smile on their face.

Until now. Something about Susannah scratched beneath the surface and left him aching.

She could dance and make love with him, then glance coolly at him as if he meant nothing to her.

Irritation coiled in his gut, interlaced with longing. He hated the power she had over him. That he lay awake at night hungering for the touch of her skin.

He'd like nothing better than to see that icy demeanor melt in the heat of desire. He enjoyed a flicker of satisfaction at the prospect of seducing her. Just because he could.

By the time he climbed the steps to the house, the setting sun bathed the land in a fiery glow that matched his mood. Inside, he pulled off his gloves. Found himself smelling the air, testing it for her presence.

She was here.

A subtle floral scent. Jasmine and a hint of citrus.

He ignored the heat and tension rising in his limbs.

No sign of her in the living room. He heard Rosa moving in the kitchen, but no sound of conversation.

He finally spotted Susannah standing on the terrace. He hesitated a moment, watching her through the closed glass doors. The red ball of the sun hung at the ridgeline of the mountains. Almost a silhouette, she stared out into the distance, slim and fragile against the harsh backdrop. A breeze pressed the skirt of her dress against her long legs.

Why did she always wear a skirt? To torment him with what he couldn't see?

He flung open the doors. "Susannah."

She spun around. Her face lit up, and a smile started to spread across it. Then she hesitated and he watched her get control of her features. "Hello, Amado."

Her big brown eyes looked up at him. Wary.

And so she should be.

He lifted her hand and kissed it, cavalier style. "The pleasure, once again, is all mine."

She flushed. Sweet. And so predictable.

She had no control over her attraction to him.

The thought gave him a vicious ripple of satisfaction. She might wish to put him behind her—a job well done—but he wouldn't let her.

Not until *he* was done with her. Which was the reason he'd left her hungry and aroused in New York. They had unfinished business.

She tucked a long lock of dark hair behind her ear. "How are your parents? I haven't seen them yet."

"My parents? You're forgetting that my mother is dead and you've just left my father in New York."

She swallowed. "I mean, Ignacio and Clara."

"They are still living." Why should he make it easy for her?

Today she wore a blue-and-white patterned dress. She favored styles from the 1930s and 1940s. Tailored jackets. Dresses fitted enough to show her slenderness, but not tight or suggestive. Necklines that revealed her delicate collarbones but nothing else.

As always, she was perfect. Irresistible. Desire swept through him like a sickness.

He took a step toward her, invading her space. "Ignacio no longer calls me 'my son' as he used to." He let his gaze linger on the curve of her cheekbone, painted pink by the setting sun.

"It must be hard."

"Yes."

Let her pure heart fill with pity for him. A sympathetic woman could be very…*giving*. And he looked forward to taking everything she had to give.

"And Clara? How is she taking it?"

"Like a mother who has lost her child."

Now, he did look away. The pained expression on Susannah's face cut to his heart. Poor Clara hadn't been herself since his true parentage came to light. Pale and harried, she kept her distance from him, ashamed by her decades-long collusion in a lie that shaped all their lives. She hadn't been to the house in a week.

"Do you think that perhaps she'd come to believe the lie? That she'd almost forgotten she didn't give birth to you?"

He frowned. "Possibly." It had never crossed his mind that Clara wasn't his true mother. She'd never betrayed a single clue.

But that was all over now. "The story's been in the papers. The gossips are whispering." He shrugged. "Nothing to be done."

He could see Susannah's overactive brain ticking away behind those soulful eyes.

"Trying to figure out how to save the day? Don't. You can't."

During dinner, Amado charmed and flirted. His earnest and thoughtful conversation, combined with wicked, sensual glances, had Susannah laughing and blushing like a schoolgirl.

She could see what he was doing—toying with her—but she couldn't seem to help her response.

He slipped out of the room after dessert to talk to Rosa, and she collapsed back in her chair, gasping for air. How did he do this to her?

Whenever she'd tried to guide the conversation in the direction of business, he'd steered it off somewhere else with a twinkle in his eye.

He had a genius for nosing out subjects she loved to talk about—places she'd visited, books she'd read, world affairs—so she was totally unable to resist engaging in heated and passionate conversation with him.

Without getting any work done.

The front door clicked shut as Rosa left. Any minute now, Amado would be back with steaming coffee. Maybe he'd offer to massage her feet? Her pulse picked up in anticipation and she cursed herself for it.

She didn't have an ounce of self-control where Amado Alvarez was concerned.

And worse, he knew it.

Instead of coffee, he returned carrying a black shawl. "Let's walk outside."

"In the dark?"

"There are many stars." Stars sparkled in his eyes.

He'd donned a dark sweater, clearly intent on going on this walk regardless of her opinion. "This'll keep you warm." He held out the fringed shawl.

"Woven from the hair of the finest local llamas?"

"Vicuñas. Their wool is softer." A smile eased up the corner of his mouth.

"I can hardly say no, then, can I?"

Amado didn't bother to reply. And why would he? They both knew she could never say no to him.

They slipped through the front door into the thick, inky night. The slight chill in the air was no match for the luscious wool wrapped around her shoulders.

No electric lights pierced the darkness. Even the large winery was invisible. "Where are Clara and Ignacio?" It felt odd that she hadn't seen them all day. They seemed to have vanished.

"How should I know?" Amado walked straight ahead. "They don't tell me everything." His voice thickened. "As you know."

Susannah clutched the shawl about her. How could the whole family fall apart, decades of love and affection dissolve into nothing, all because of the news *she* brought?

Even though she knew she wasn't to blame, her chest ached with guilt and the painful longing to put things right.

The slim sickle of moon gave little light. Amado strode so fast she had to hurry to keep up with him.

"Where are we going?"

"To visit a friend."

The brusque answer was a stark contrast to his calculated charm at dinner. Susannah got breathless trying to keep up. Her medium heels weren't ideal for half-running across gravel, and now a rather crooked brick walkway.

She stumbled and almost lost her balance, which caused Amado to turn and frown at her. He glanced down at her feet.

"Yes, I'm wearing heels. I didn't realize there'd be a midnight trek involved."

"Usually you wear more sensible shoes." There was a hint of a question in his voice.

"Not always," she protested. She didn't want him to know that she'd bought new shoes especially for the visit. Her feet had remembered the lavish care and attention he'd paid them last time. "Besides, your vineyard is so well maintained, I didn't even bother to bring boots this time."

"You should have. What if it rains?"

He held her forearms. Her skin hummed under the firm pressure of his fingers and thumbs.

"Maybe I wasn't feeling sensible." Her breasts tingled as the confession slipped out of her.

"It's important to be sensible on a business trip." His eyes glinted in the darkness. "And this is a business trip for you, isn't it?"

"Yes." She swallowed. All her insecurities bubbled to the surface like scum. "I realize you probably didn't want to see me again. I understand that. I brought unwelcome news that has changed your life. I didn't ask to come."

She wobbled in her new shoes.

Amado held her forearms tighter. "No. *I* asked for you to come."

"You did?" Her mouth fell open. "But I thought… Tarrant…"

"Oh, he has his own reasons for your being here, no doubt. But I asked him to send you."

A shiver of nameless emotion rippled through her. "Why?"

"Because I could."

He let go of her arms, turned, and marched forward into the velvet darkness.

Susannah stared after him, mouth gaping. Her heart pounded and indignant protests rose to her tongue. She'd cancelled a long-planned trip so that two wealthy men could trade her around like a party favor?

"Come on."

She heard his voice receding. She turned to assess the distance back to the house, but it was impossible to even see it in the tarry blackness of the night.

High above, the stars winked at her, mocking.

She hurried after him.

Soft light appeared in a doorway. She pulled the shawl tight around her and followed him inside.

A barn. A caged light fixture illuminated a clean wooden floor. She smelled hay, fresh and slightly sweet.

She walked slowly, keeping her heels light on the floor.

"This way." Amado's voice drew her around a corner. Rows of horse stalls with elegant wrought iron gratings lined the wide aisle. She could hear animals shifting, feet moving.

He pulled back a sliding door and stepped into a stall. "Come in."

Susannah walked up to the stall and looked through the bars. A giant brown horse appeared in the gloom. She hesitated. Enormous animals made her uneasy.

Amado was bent over in a far corner of the large stall. The horse lifted its magnificent head and peered down at her with disdain.

She shrank back. "It's okay, I'll wait here."

Amado looked up. "You're afraid?"

She inhaled and lifted her chin. Amado rose and crossed the stall. "Perhaps I should have started with a formal introduction. Susannah, this is Tierra de Oro's Andrómeda, known to her friends as Luz. Luz, this is Susannah Clarke."

Susannah couldn't help smiling. "What do I do now, shake her hoof?"

Amado made a sound with his tongue and Luz lifted one of her front feet.

She had to laugh. "You're good with animals."

"She trusts me." He flashed a wicked grin, and stroked Luz's vast neck. "Maybe you should do the same?"

Susannah gulped. Determined not to appear chicken, she squeezed past the door and closed it behind her. Then she noticed the baby, small and gangly with a tuft of white mane, in a gloomy corner of the stall.

"How cute. How old is it?" She glanced nervously up at Luz, then walked around her.

"Luna is three days old." Amado held his hand out for the tiny foal to sniff. "She's just getting used to me."

"Her mother doesn't mind?"

"Oh, no. She's known me since she was born. And this is her sixth baby, so she knows the routine."

Susannah's stomach tightened with strange force as she saw how gentle he was with the nervous baby. The mother blew out a snort of air that made Susannah jump. Amado didn't even look up.

"Do you want to come touch her?" He had his arms wrapped around the foal's slender chest.

"That's okay, thanks. I'm enjoying watching."

He didn't press her any further. She looked sideways at Luz, feeling like a wimp. The mother horse ignored her completely.

Amado touched the baby all over, his gaze soft and his

touch obviously light. The foal seemed to relax under his hands, and lowered its delicate honey-colored head.

"I try to come out here at least three times a day." He spoke softly. "So she'll get to know me and know I mean her no harm."

"That's nice." She had no idea what else to say.

Amado glanced up. Laughed. "Didn't you grow up in the country?"

"Yes, but I never had anything to do with animals. I helped out with schools, counseling programs, stuff like that."

"Oh." His eyes twinkled. "Do you like animals?"

"Sure," she said uncertainly. She had a feeling this was some kind of test. She wanted very badly to pass it.

Why? What did it matter if Amado thought she was an uptight city girl?

She crossed her arms over her chest. Pretended not to watch as Amado murmured softly to the foal. Tried to ignore the strange fluttery feeling his tender behavior sent to her stomach.

Luz turned and lowered her big head onto Susannah's shoulder. Startled, she used every ounce of energy she could muster to remain completely still. Luz blew out a breath that warmed her cheek.

Susannah glanced sideways without moving. Luz's large brown eye regarded her calmly.

"She's telling you to relax." Amado didn't even look up.

"It's working." Susannah raised her arm and patted Luz awkwardly on the neck.

Out of the corner of her eye, she saw Amado smile.

A sense of warm satisfaction crept over her.

Amado rose and fondled Luz affectionately before following her out into the aisle and closing the door.

"What will happen to the baby?" Susannah waited until

they were out of the horse's earshot before asking. That was probably laughable in itself.

Amado looked at her strangely. "What do you mean?"

"Will you sell her?"

"Probably. We'd have a lot of horses if we kept the foals born every year. My dad…" He cleared his throat. "Ignacio has always bred horses. His father before him. It's a tradition, I suppose."

"But you seem so attached to her already. How do you get used to it? Saying goodbye and moving on?"

Amado frowned slightly. "You know all about moving on. It's part of life."

"Yes." Silence thickened in the air, punctuated only by the sound of animals moving. Breathing. "Of course."

Amado continued along the aisle, past a number of stalls. She'd seen workers riding the horses around the *estancia,* checking the nets that shielded the grapes from hail and repairing the trellis that held the vines upright.

Horses were quieter and more beautiful than the usually ubiquitous ATVs. Easier on the earth, too.

A strange thought occurred to her. "And the father. Is he here too?"

Amado's expression darkened. "What do you mean?"

"The sire of Luna."

"No. He lives a few kilometers away at my friend Diego's place. We bring him here to cover her."

"So, he may not even know he's a father."

"No, and I don't suppose he cares either. He had his fun."

"Like Tarrant Hardcastle." The words echoed in the cool, clean, dim barn aisle.

Susannah bit her tongue. She could hardly believe she'd said that aloud.

Amado stiffened. "What are you trying to say?"

"That this foal has two fathers. One who gave it life, and another who'll raise it. And that's okay. Things will settle down and your life will get back to normal."

She realized she was trying to convince herself as much as him. Tears pricked her eyelids. Even though she knew she shouldn't, she felt horribly responsible for the state of unrest at Tierra de Oro.

He lifted his eyes and stared at her. A look so fierce it stole her breath.

They stood underneath the single bulb, whose harsh light emphasized the proud planes of his face.

"What business is it of yours? You can go back to your travels and forget all about us. You have no reason to care."

"But I do care."

Her high voice rang off the polished wood of the stalls, off the wrought iron and the wood and stone floor.

Her heart squeezed in her chest. Amado's features were rigid, but emotion churned in the black depths of his eyes. Already he meant too much to her.

Far too much.

It took a tiny fraction of a second for their bodies to collide and their lips to come together. Inevitable.

Eight

Amado took Susannah in his arms with force. Her fingers reached, instinctively, for the solid muscle of his back. The shawl fell to the floor, but his arms were warmer.

They stumbled into some kind of storage room, piled almost to the ceiling with hay on one side. Amado spread a blanket out over a mattress of bales, and eased her onto it, all without removing his arm from around her waist.

The heat of his body excited her, even through his clothes. She slid her hands under his shirt and explored the smooth, powerful surface of his back. He unbuttoned the front of her dress to expose her bra. He paused, blinked, and sighed with pleasure.

His unembarrassed desire made passion unfurl in Susannah's belly. She found herself writhing against him. Inviting him to go further.

She unbuckled his leather belt and slid his pants down

to reveal his fierce arousal. He lifted her skirt and ran his hands over her bare thighs. The rough texture of his palms and fingers sent shivers of awareness darting through her.

Her breath quickened as Amado's hands explored the silky surface of her panties. She tugged him close until his hardness jutted against her.

"I want you inside me." She breathed the words in his ear. Urgent.

He lowered her swiftly onto the blanket, and she sank into the hay-cushioned surface. Amado climbed over her, his face taut with passion.

He opened his eyes for a second. Black and filled with emotion, his gaze met hers. Then he pushed up her dress, slid her panties down over her shivering legs, and entered her.

An exclamation slipped from her mouth. Crude relief. He kissed her face, layering hard, passionate kisses over her mouth and cheeks.

"I missed you," she murmured, unable to stop herself.

"I missed you, too." His breath was hot on her face, his movements agitated with excitement. She wriggled under him, taking him deeper.

Raw emotion cascaded through her, tightening her muscles and making her cling to him. She'd ached for him. Longed for him.

What did it matter that he knew?

She kissed his face all over, as they moved in rhythmic bliss. Her insides throbbed as he penetrated deeper and deeper, running his hands over her arms and touching her face. Stroking her hair, his breathing unsteady and his eyes closed tight.

I love you, Amado.

The words exploded into her brain in a rush. She managed not to say them but it took every ounce of self-control.

Proof that she still had some left. Somewhere.

Adrenaline crashed through her. Urgent, she switched positions with him, clumsy and needy, until she was on top.

She rode him, fast and hard, trying to get control of the sensations and emotions wringing through her.

His hands on her breasts drove her deeper into a fog of delicious arousal. His thumbs played over her nipples until they were supersensitive and rock hard inside her bra.

She could hear herself moaning, whispering, as her climax approached. She touched his face, his hard, high cheekbones and strong jaw. She felt his thick, soft hair and the roping muscles of his neck.

Oh, Amado. She said it aloud. Or at least she thought she did. The veil between dream and reality was so thin it was hard to tell.

Right when she was about to let go, he took control again. Lifted his back until he sat facing her, cradling her in his lap as he throbbed deep inside her.

Arms and legs intertwined, they kissed. Restrained, slow and sensual. The graze of teeth on a cheek, the lick of hot tongue over closed lips.

Amado held her totally still, unable to move although she was almost ready to explode. Desire pulsed through her, shaking her limbs and squeezing her inner muscles into a state of near-convulsion.

His self-control seemed total as he held them together, moving—slow and deep—inside her.

Tension swelled in the air and in their bodies as the need for release built beyond their ability to endure it. Susannah rocked, just once, then a fiery explosion ripped through her.

Amado's climax followed, as they clung to each other, face-to-face.

When she opened her eyes, she realized that tears were streaming down her cheeks.

Amado held her close, eyes closed.

How could she not love him?

She loved his passion for his estate and the fine wines it produced. She loved his deep feelings for the people and even the animals around him.

She loved his insight into her character, and that he'd found another side of her that she never knew existed. The hitherto unknown and unexplored territory of Susannah Clarke that was capable of soul-shaking passion.

Here there be dragons.

She'd never dared to tap into her sensual side before. Her upbringing had warned her repeatedly of the treacherous quagmire of lust that could draw you from the world of responsibility and commitment into a realm of licentious and wasteful pleasure.

But Amado had taken her there and she'd found it to be a lush, rich place that felt totally natural and healthy.

Except for the part where she'd slept with her boss's son. While visiting on business.

She bit her lip.

And the reality that this relationship had no future, because he was here and she was in New York. When she even was in New York.

"You're thinking again." Amado's soft voice penetrated the web of anxiety closing over her.

"How can you tell?" She tried to sound lighthearted.

"You get this tiny wrinkle between your eyebrows." His dark eyes sparkled.

"Sounds ugly."

He shook his head. "It's a beautiful wrinkle." He leaned forward and kissed between her brows. The touch of his lips was so soft it made her catch her breath. "But you know by now that there's a time for thinking and a time for just being."

He withdrew from her and settled her onto the blanket. Spread another soft blanket over her, then removed the condom.

Condom? She didn't even remember him putting it on. Lucky one of them had a brain. Maybe this lust thing was a quicksand to disaster after all. She'd end up pregnant like Marisa Alvarez and...

The sound of laughter made her look up. "That pretty wrinkle is showing again."

She sucked in a shaky breath. Amado lifted the blanket and slid underneath it. She couldn't help welcoming his warm body next to hers. Wrapping her arms around him and holding him close.

If only they could stay like this forever and...

A breathy, snorting sound made her jump.

"Relax, it's one of the horses."

Susannah blinked. "We're in the barn."

Amado shot her a perplexed look. "Of course."

A flush spread over her face. "Did the horses hear...you know?"

"Perhaps you should ask them." His mouth curved into a smile.

He didn't seem at all freaked out by the fact that they'd just made love in a *stable*. What kind of madwoman was he turning her into?

Then again, maybe he did this all the time. The blankets were conveniently here. He had a condom with him, for crying out loud.

Maybe he left a stash of them handy for such rustic

trysts? No doubt the romantic cliché of love in a hayloft was a big hit with the tourists.

Her heart stung with pain at the thought of him making love to another woman.

Amado ran his thumb over the spot between her eyebrows, smoothing that pesky wrinkle.

She couldn't bring herself to open her eyes and look at him. To see that admiring and sensual gaze he no doubt bestowed on many lucky women each year.

"What are we going to do with you? I'll have to punish you for thinking too much."

"I bet there are some whips handy in the tack room." She kept her voice light. And her eyes shut tight.

Amado laughed. "I'm just a country boy. I don't know about that kinky stuff."

"How do you know if you've never tried?" She cracked her eyes open a tiny bit.

Amado's serious expression made her laugh. He looked downright worried.

"I'm kidding. Relax. Now you're thinking too much. I'm probably the least kinky person on the planet." She looked at him. "Or at least I thought I was until I met you."

"You're a very passionate woman." He squeezed her. Pulled her even closer until her chest rested against his. "Affectionate, too. I like that." He pressed a warm kiss to her cheek.

Her dress was still unbuttoned and crumpled around her, but she couldn't summon the energy to care.

She was affectionate. And passionate. She let the pleasant thoughts rest in her tired brain. And she liked Amado Alvarez very much.

She couldn't *love* him.

She heard her breathing catch.

Amado leaned forward and pressed a gentle kiss to her famous wrinkle.

But I like him very much.

In the morning, Susannah woke up alone on the hay, still wrapped in blankets. No sign of Amado.

Light poured through a crack in the door, and she realized she'd been awakened by the sound of voices.

Male voices. Neither of them Amado's.

"Here, stirring up trouble again." She froze. Listened to a snort of disgust. "You'd think she'd be ashamed to show her face. It's not enough for her to destroy our family. Now she has to come back and meddle in our business affairs?"

The angry one was Ignacio. Susannah shrank into the hay, trying not to breathe lest she give away her hiding place.

She glanced around. The sliding door to the hay storage room was closed. Amado must have done that on his way out. She wondered if he intended to preserve her modesty or keep her his prisoner.

The second voice was less expressive. "Yes…of course…it's true." The platitudes of an employee who doesn't want to ruffle the boss's already prickly feathers.

Susannah glanced down at the hay-covered blanket, then put a hand in her own hair. She so did not want to know what she looked like right now. It was clearly broad daylight and people were up and about.

How could Amado leave her here like this? Did he want her to be discovered so she could be a subject of gossip and derision?

Her blood chilled.

Maybe he did. He'd obviously summoned her here for

some purpose of his own, and he might have an agenda broader than simple sex.

A baser motive, like *revenge*.

The voices had receded to the far end of the large barn. She wriggled out of the blanket and hastily buttoned the front of her dress. One of the blue buttons was missing and the collar was hopelessly crumpled, as was the full skirt. If anyone saw her…

She had to make sure no one did.

She eased off the pile of hay bales and rolled up the blankets. Stuck them in a corner.

A nervous grope proved that her hair was a tangled mess. She tried to shake out any loose grass stems, then she picked up her fallen shoes and tiptoed toward the door.

She held her breath as she lifted the metal ring that served as a handle and gave a tug. The door didn't budge.

Her blood pressure shot up. Could he really mean to trap her here? To make her call for help?

Or simply to cool her heels until such time as he had need of her again.

Her breathing grew audible. Maybe she could pick the lock? If she could figure out what kind of lock it was. Most likely a simple latch…

Footsteps headed back down the aisle. She shrank away from the door and pressed herself against the wall.

"The boss is going crazy. This New York chick is the final straw." It sounded like the previously taciturn employee, turned garrulous.

And another voice. "Clara is even more nuts. She hasn't spoken to him for days. I tried to find out why from Rosa but she threatened to whack me with her frying pan if I talked about her beloved master and mistress."

The other clucked his tongue. "I saw Amado galloping

off like a madman this morning. Heading for the mountains like the devil was chasing him. The whole place is going to go to hell."

"My mom said they had it coming." She heard the sound of a bucket being filled with water. "You can't live with a lie. Sooner or later it will sneak out and bite you."

"Your mom talks too much."

"You'd better eat those words before I…" The conversation devolved into a good-natured and shockingly crude exchange that made Susannah blush.

She glanced back at the hay and her face heated further.

How on earth could she get out of here now? No window. The door locked.

She could barely recall any of the tender feelings she'd had for Amado last night. Right now, she'd like to wrap her fingers around his neck and—

The door slid open and slammed into its cradle with a crash. A man strode into the room, picked up a bale of hay by the strings, turned to exit and…

Stared right at her.

"Dios mio." A kid of about nineteen, eyes on stalks.

"Hi."

"I didn't hear you." He hitched the hay bale higher. Looked ready to make a dash for the door.

"I came to get some hay." She cleared her throat. "And I got locked in."

He glanced at the shoes in her hand. "The door wasn't locked."

Susannah swallowed hard. "Oh. I guess it got stuck." She forced out a foolish cackle. "Then, I'll be on my way."

He glanced at the blankets in the corner and a smirk crept across his face. She wished she could crawl right under a hay bale and die, but instead she held her head high and marched right past him.

She made it back to her bedroom. More accurately, Marisa's room, which still had ruffled chiffon curtains from the 1970s. The sight of herself in the mirror, hair wild, clothes rumpled and eyes glazed with passion, only made her cringe more.

Now they *really* had something to talk about around here.

She glanced at a framed portrait of Marisa, which stood on a delicate white dressing table. Dark and striking with long, wavy hair and a striped T-shirt, she was a finer-boned, feminine version of Amado. Easy to see how he'd assumed she was his sister.

Laughing in the photo, she waved at the camera.

Susannah's heart clenched as her own petty concerns shrank into perspective. This lovely young woman faced up to the challenges of motherhood, but never got a chance to taste its joys.

What would you do, Marisa? She felt a sudden sense of responsibility to the woman whose old room she stood in and whose son she had such strange and strong feelings for.

In that instant, she made up her mind about one thing. She'd had enough of people blaming her for breaking up this family and she was going to do something about putting it back together.

Showered and changed, wearing sensible flats and a conservative pantsuit, Susannah grabbed one of the pastries left on the dining room table.

No sign whatsoever of Amado, which was not surprising given what she'd overheard. She faked a cheerful smile for Rosa—who might or might not have seen her creeping into the house like a thief—and marched out the front door. Even the dogs were nowhere to be seen.

Since she wasn't sure exactly where Clara and Ignacio's new house was, she drove to the winery building and asked. Worried stares followed her as she climbed back in the rental car and drove along a pretty, landscaped driveway to a striking modern house with a view of the mountains.

She knocked on the polished door and her heart battered against her ribs as she waited until footsteps on the other side grew closer. Finally, Clara pulled the door open, inhaled sharply at the sight of her, and slammed it.

"Please, I just want to talk to you." She tapped on the door with her knuckles. "Woman to woman."

She waited. No movement on the other side of the door. Which meant that Clara was still standing there.

After a painful wait, she heard the chrome handle turn. "Come in." The older woman ushered her into a bright, clean space. Comfortable, solid furniture gathered around a central fireplace, and bright rugs decorated the tiled floor.

Susannah didn't waste words in idle compliments. "I haven't come to apologize, because I only did what I was asked to do, and it's no crime."

Clara frowned.

"But I have come to implore you to heal the rift in your household." She stepped toward Clara. "You're the center of the family, and nothing that has happened changes that. You're the wife and mother of the men in your life, regardless of how you came to that role. It's your duty to keep the family together."

She paused for breath, blinking. She hadn't rehearsed, but simply spoke her mind. As Clara stared at her, blue eyes wide, Susannah reflected that her words must sound pretty arrogant coming from a single woman living a thousand miles from her own family.

That didn't seem to stop her though. "I know you're a woman of great strength. You've raised two children and helped care for this estate for over forty years. It doesn't make sense to me that you'd give up now and let everything you've built and nurtured crumble to dust."

Tears sparkled in Clara's eyes. "I never liked the pretense. It pained me. But Ignacio was so devastated by the death of his only child, especially after losing his wife." A tear rolled down her weathered cheek. "And I…I loved him so much."

Clara pulled a much-used handkerchief out of her pocket and dabbed at her eyes. "I'd already loved that man for years. Adored him like a fool. I was no beauty. I had no education or family. I never dared to dream that a man like Ignacio Alvarez would ask his housekeeper to marry him. And when he did—" She drew in a ragged breath. "I couldn't say no."

Susannah hesitated for a moment, frozen by the emotion pulsing in the quiet room. Then she stepped forward and placed her hand on Clara's solid shoulder. "You did the right thing. You created a family for Amado, welcomed him into your heart. He is your son, you both know that."

"I have no son. And my husband only married me to prevent a scandal." A painful laugh ripped from her mouth. "And now the gossips are braying louder than ever. My whole life is a fraud."

"That's not true. You raised Amado. You're his mother. Nothing can *ever* change that." She drew in a shaky breath. "And your husband needs you."

"I'm a foolish old woman. No one needs me."

"You're Ignacio's wife. Regardless of the circumstance

of your marriage, you promised to support and comfort him. You rose to the challenge of doing that after Amado was born, and you must do it again."

Clara peered at her, tears glittering in her eyes. "I've tried my best to be a good wife to him. And he's been a good husband to me."

"And what makes you think you can stop now? Just because the 'secret' is out? Maybe your life got harder, but that doesn't mean you get to give up on it. Your husband and son need you more than ever."

Clara drew in a deep breath. "You show a lot of wisdom for someone so young."

"I'm not that young." Susannah squeezed her arm. She felt strangely calm. "And I learned from my parents who counseled a lot of people over the years. Everyone needs advice sometimes, including me."

"And I'd be a foolish old woman not to listen." Clara reached into her pocket for a fresh handkerchief, and wiped her cheeks. "Come have some coffee."

Buzzing on Clara's strong coffee, Susannah left the house with increased determination to find Ignacio and sort out this mess. She spotted him striding among some older rows of Cabernet, so she abandoned the car and struck out across the field.

"Mr. Alvarez!" She tried to sound friendly.

He turned and a scowl darkened his face at the sight of her. "Haven't you done enough harm?"

"That's why I want to talk to you. There's no reason for you all to be at odds."

"Why not? Our entire existence is based on a false-hood. One *I* initiated, as my 'wife' so acutely points out." Bitterness darkened his voice.

"You did what you thought was right."

"Bah. I did what my pride dictated. I didn't want people to know that my daughter had a baby out of wedlock. She was right to be afraid to tell me she was pregnant. I would *not* have been understanding. So, see? I am largely responsible for her death, as well." His silvery-gray brows lowered over steely eyes, challenging her to find the silver lining in *that*.

Susannah hesitated. "Your wife loves you very much." She spoke softly.

He peered at her. "My wife? The woman I married to preserve what was left of my family honor. If anything, I exploited her. Hired her for a new role, much as your boss *Mr. Tarrant Hardcastle* hired you for yours." He spat the name like a sour pit.

He shook his head. "I promised my first wife—as she lay dying after giving birth to Marisa—that I'd never marry again. Yet I did, for purely practical purposes. To maintain my dignity. Clara has every right to hate me for stealing her life."

Susannah dug her toe into the soft dirt. "But that marriage of convenience grew into love." She looked down as she said it. Not wanting to embarrass Ignacio with the sentiment and drive him further away.

After the second cup of coffee, she'd asked Clara point blank if they were a husband and wife in every sense. Clara had colored and admitted that, yes, they did enjoy "intimacy." That over the years she'd almost totally forgotten the businesslike arrangement she'd first agreed to.

"What do you know of love?" Ignacio stared her down. "You, a girl who wanders the world, flitting from one place to another at whim. What do you know of family? Of a legacy carefully nourished for over a century, now shattered?"

"But it doesn't have to be shattered." She couldn't help stepping forward. How did he know so much about her? Had Amado spoken of her? "Amado is your son because you raised him. He's also your grandson, and your biological heir through Marisa."

Ignacio lifted his broad chin. "We all know exactly where we stand, thanks to you and your puppet master, Mr. Tarrant Hardcastle." His eyes narrowed. "And Tierra de Oro would *never* consider doing business with the man who casually ruined my daughter and destroyed her life."

Susannah flinched away from his fierce emotion. It hadn't occurred to her that Ignacio would be dead set against doing business with Tarrant. Maybe she was too used to working for a company where profits trumped all other considerations.

"We'd be a lot better off if you'd leave Tierra de Oro and *never* return."

He turned and walked away.

Susannah stood looking after him, heart pounding. She blew out a breath. It probably would have been better if she'd never come.

Who was she kidding? Of course it would have.

She intentionally left her car behind and stomped along the rows of vines back to the winery, pain streaking through her. Maybe it was time to show some spine and leave them alone. Let Tarrant fire her if he must.

Her cell vibrated in her jacket pocket. "Hello."

"Meet me at the winery in half an hour." Click.

Amado hung up immediately after issuing the brusque command. So different from the tender and thoughtful lover of last night.

Irritation at his high-handed attitude dissolved into sadness that trickled down her spine. Everything was so wonderful when it was just the two of them, alone in the dark when the world faded away into obscurity. In his arms, she transformed into a stronger, more daring and demanding person.

In the harsh light of day, however, she was left with an ache that wouldn't go away. A hunger that couldn't be satisfied by food. She'd never felt so alone.

She squinted in the midday sun. She was right outside the big winery building already, so she decided to go in and poke around.

Nine

Amado strode along the road from the house, steam pouring off him. His gallop in the hills had done nothing to ease the tension creeping through his limbs. He'd showered and scrubbed and changed, trying to wash off any emotion that still lingered from last night along with the sticky-sweet smell of sex.

But already he craved Susannah again. Not just her lithe, sensuous body and long silky hair, but her warm curiosity, her thoughtful insight, even that damn wrinkle between her slim, arched brows.

Part of him wanted to send her packing with nothing. No deal, no wine, no contracts and no further connection between Tierra de Oro and Hardcastle Enterprises and its big-shot owner.

But another part of him wanted to hold her tight in his arms, kiss her until her lips flushed dark, make love to her until she cried out with the force of her release.

The second part was winning.

He shoved open the ten-foot-high oak door and marched into the winery building. The tasting room, where he expected Susannah to wait for him, was empty.

So was the barrel room. Several wines were being transferred from vats to new barrels today, but there was no sign of activity.

He walked toward the crushing room. The busiest part of the winery at harvest time, when it welcomed box after box of fresh hand-picked grapes. Right now, however, the big crushing machines were silent, waiting for the grapes to mature.

A burst of laughter drew him through the empty room and out into the blinding sunshine.

A group huddled around the upturned barrels where his employees gathered for breaks. In their midst sat Susannah, incongruously dressed in a pair of white overalls liberally stained with fresh red grape juice.

She stopped laughing when she saw him. "Hi, Amado. Sofia and Joaquín are showing me how to drink *maté*."

Sofia passed Susannah the steaming gourd of brewed tea. Susannah lifted it to her mouth and took a sip through the *bombilla*.

He ignored the heat that crept through him as he watched her lips close delicately around the familiar metal straw.

She glanced up at him with those dark, yearning eyes. "Would you like some?"

He strode forward and snatched the gourd. Sipped, his mind distracted by the innocent pout of her lips.

The *maté* tasted mild. They must have poured several cups of hot water over the leaves by now. Not that he needed a jolt of energy. If anything, he had far too much.

He passed the gourd to Joaquín and frowned at Susannah's getup.

"Tomás showed me how to clean the inside of a vat. I hope you don't mind. I didn't slow them down too much."

Big, friendly Tomás laughed. "Slow us down? You should hire her full-time. She's a pro."

Amado nodded. The sight of Susannah in those white workers' overalls was having a very disturbing effect on him. He wondered what she wore underneath. The red wine stains matched her mobile lips, and the dark spots of color high on her cheeks.

"Susannah and I have work to do," he muttered.

He turned and strode back into the building, gratified to hear the sound of Susannah's rubber boots squeaking after him.

How did she have such power over him? A tide of exasperation rose in his blood along with the throb of desire. He'd woken this morning in a lather of lust and contentment, wrapped like a swaddled babe in Susannah's arms.

He could have stayed there all day, listening to her heartfelt opinions and basking in the glow of curiosity and enthusiasm that lit her eyes.

It took a tremendous amount of self-control to extricate himself, and even then he hadn't dared to wake her in case those big, dark eyes flickering open undermined his last ounce of will.

He flung open the door to his office.

"I should probably change. I might get wine on something."

"This is a winery. It won't be a problem." He tried not to look at the way the white cotton pulled tight over her slim thighs as she sat.

"I really enjoyed seeing how they move the wine from

a vat to the barrels. Your staff are experts. And they love their work. Where do you find them?"

He rustled through some papers. "I offer internships to students of winemaking from various schools around the world. Some of them have turned into my best employees. And of course, hard-working local people are the backbone of our business."

He glanced up. Susannah sat in her chair, glowing. Was she not even angry that he'd left her alone in the barn?

She didn't seem at all put out. She looked quite at home in *his* winery, laughing and drinking *maté* with his workers like she'd been here for years.

He found he wanted a reaction from her. Any reaction.

"Do you interrupt the work at every winery you visit, or only when you've slept with the owner?"

Her mouth fell open. Then snapped shut. "I...they offered to let me help. If I did something wrong, I'm sorry. And they said they always drink *maté* in the afternoon. I've seen people drink it before, and always wanted to try it. There's something about sharing the drink that makes it so different from the way we consume most things these days."

He leaned back in his chair. "I'd imagine an American would think it unhygienic."

She shrugged. "I think it's beautiful."

He ignored the sensation tightening his chest. *What a load of sentimental rubbish.* "You should advise Tarrant Hardcastle to open the world's most exclusive *maté* café."

She laughed. "That wouldn't be the same at all."

"Still, now that you've looked around, I imagine you have some ideas for how to improve our winery."

He stared at her, challenging her to find fault with the business he'd nourished with his life's blood.

She licked her lips, which sent an unfortunate flare of

heat to his groin. "The operation itself is state of the art. Obviously, a lot of thought went into the layout and equipment, and the staff seem ideal." She hesitated.

"But?" His voice emerged as a growl.

"I could make some suggestions to enhance your marketing. Improving the labeling and adding focus to the brand impression, if you're interested." She fiddled with a button on the front of her overalls—his overalls—looking nervous.

"Oh, I'm *very* interested." He leaned back in his chair.

"Well, it's just that the label doesn't suggest a real identity for the vineyard, or for the wine."

"It has our name on it."

"Yes, but marketing wine today is a lot about image. One image says young, hip and fresh, and another says ancient and venerable."

Amado drummed his fingers on the arm of his chair. "And what image springs to mind when you visualize Tierra de Oro?"

That wrinkle appeared between her brows. She tilted her head back and stared at the ceiling for a moment. Then, she lowered her head and leveled that steady brown gaze at him. "Simplicity."

He scowled. "Simplicity? We may seem like simple nobodies to an office in New York, but I assure you that both our wines and our operations are highly complex."

She leaned forward. "That's not what I mean at all." She picked up a bottle of 2006 Syrah that was sitting on the desk. "There's magic here, in the light, in the mountains, in the fact that you've tended and cherished the same land for one hundred years. This rather busy label with a generic pattern of grape leaves doesn't convey that."

He tapped his fingernails together. Arched a brow. Tried

to drag his focus from her closed mouth. "And what exactly do you suggest?"

"A lighter color, maybe unbleached paper, with a pale graphic image of the mountains, perhaps. Crisp writing."

He could visualize it. Not bad.

"And your winery building is dramatic and beautiful."

Amado crossed his arms over this chest, unable to resist a swell of pride. He'd designed the building himself, with the help of a close friend who'd studied architecture. "It was built using the ancient stonemasonry techniques of the Huarpe people."

"So, it's something unique and special to Tierra de Oro. It expresses the character of the vineyard and its wines. You could print an image of it along the bottom of the label."

Amado frowned. "Hmm. I see your point."

"And you could extend it to other items for guests at the vineyard. T-shirts, tote bags, perhaps even a simple wine rack and items of that nature."

He snorted. "This is not a Disney World theme park. And we have T-shirts."

Susannah winced slightly. "Those bright blue ones? They look like they're advertising a local election."

Irritation at the insult rose inside him, but he couldn't help laughing. "Ignacio ran for local office a few years ago, and we did purchase a large batch of shirts and used them for both."

Susannah's sensual mouth tilted into a smile as she tried not to laugh. She leaned back and crossed her arms. "The vineyard deserves its own unique brand. You've gone far on the quality of your wines alone, but to penetrate markets in the U.S. it'll help to have a more distinctive style."

He hated to admit she was probably right. Decided not to. "Where are your clothes?"

"Back there, actually." She tilted her head toward his office bathroom with its attached changing room. "I changed here. I hope you don't mind."

"Not in the least. I only wish I was here to watch." He waited for her reaction.

She gazed at him steadily. "Why did you leave me alone in the barn?"

"I had business to take care of."

"One of your workers found me there."

He sat upright as guilt snaked through him. "Who?"

"I don't know. A kid in a blue winery T-shirt." She shrugged. "I just thought I should warn you."

Great. It was probably Rosa's great-grandson Nahuel, whose lips flapped even more than hers.

But Susannah still didn't look embarrassed. Those dark eyes were cool and appraising. Perhaps studying him for faults and areas for improvement, much as she'd examined his estate.

No doubt leaving her in the barn was one of those. He'd done it to regain control over his body and mind. "I have no interest in idle gossip, and I assume you don't, either."

Her long, dark hair was falling from a loose knot, tumbling around her high cheekbones to her slim shoulders, and he longed to push his fingers into its softness.

Control? Only so long as he wasn't anywhere near her.

"I spoke to Clara." She frowned and shoved a lock of hair behind her ear. "I tried to reassure her that nothing has truly changed. I think I succeeded. She loves Ignacio very much."

Her audacity astonished him. Who was she to stick her

finger into a bleeding wound? "You should stay out of our family business."

"That's what Ignacio said when I spoke to him." She licked her lips, which sent heat spiking through his groin.

He cursed silently. "Stay away from him. You have no idea what you're doing."

Amado wasn't sure he could ever forgive Ignacio for driving away the woman he loved. Feelings he'd kept locked away for a decade scratched at him now, raw and painful.

It was Susannah's fault. Not only because she'd exploded a bomb in his family's midst.

Worse, her warm caresses and heartfelt passion reached inside him to dig up the sharp, broken pieces of his heart.

She had awakened sensations and longings he'd forgotten. Jolted to life areas of his body and mind that he'd thought permanently shattered by a woman who'd said she loved him, but had left him anyway.

"Ignacio said I should leave immediately."

His gut tightened. "Your boss wouldn't like that."

"No." Her eyes searched his face. "And I wouldn't, either. I want to bring your wines to the States. I'm sure they'll acquire an excellent reception. Your prices could increase quite dramatically with some critical acclaim."

Amado leaned back in his chair. Drew in a slow, silent breath. He couldn't deny that the prospect appealed to him, partly because it would assert his independence from the man who lied to him for thirty years. Who'd distorted his life and driven Valentina out of it.

He refused to let Ignacio run Susannah off the estate. He wasn't ready to lose her. Not yet. Not until he was finished with her.

It infuriated him that she seemed to think she could run his life. That she knew how to sell his wines better than he did. That she thought she could bring news that shattered his family, then glue them all back together and stick a pretty bow on top.

But she wasn't in control. He could seduce her right now, right here, and she wouldn't refuse.

That gave him a grim sense of satisfaction. And also aroused a mess of feelings he didn't even begin to know how to examine.

"Perhaps you should get dressed."

"I guess so." She glanced down at the stained overalls. "Though I rather like wearing wine."

He couldn't help smiling. And watching closely as she stood and stretched those long, lean limbs. She glanced over her shoulder as she entered the large bathroom, which had a spacious changing area. He often used it to clean up before a group of guests arrived. The wide sofa would provide a soft and comfortable surface for...

Who was in danger of losing control here? He blew out a hard breath and sprung from his chair. Maybe it would be better if Susannah went back to New York as soon as possible. Her presence was a distraction. Already his name was on the lips of gossips and scandalmongers, he didn't need them to get started on this brief and inconsequential affair.

"What should I do with these?" She held the stained overalls out through a crack in the door.

His eyes narrowed. He strode across the room and snatched them from her hands. Unfortunately, he couldn't help glimpsing a flash of silky, bare skin in skimpy, lace-trimmed underwear.

Arousal flashed through him like heat lightning.

He entered the changing room and closed the door behind him. Susannah's eyes widened. Her thick lashes lowered for a second in a display of modesty.

But her nipples, peaked beneath her silky, champagne-colored bra, made a mockery of her reserve.

He ran his palm over the dip in her waist. Her belly contracted at his touch. He marveled at the way her body responded to his—every time.

Thoughtful and sharp, Susannah couldn't help also being sensual, instinctive.

He heard her breathing quicken. "Why did you really leave me alone in the barn?"

"I had work to do."

"You could have woken me."

"I didn't want to disturb you." He held her gaze. Pictured her waking up, alone. Searching for him.

His arousal quickened.

"I was worried. I thought maybe…" She bit her lip.

"What?"

She flicked a dark glance at him. "I couldn't open the door. I thought you locked me in."

He laughed. "Keeping you my prisoner until such time as I should have need of you again?"

She smiled. "It sounds silly, doesn't it? I guess I panicked."

"Still, it's not a bad idea." He turned and flicked the lock on the door. "I do like having you at my disposal."

"Ignacio was in the barn, too."

He froze. "He saw you?"

"No, he was gone by the time the boy found me. But he could find out. I don't want to cause any more trouble."

She looked so earnest, standing there in her expensive underwear.

Life was full of cruel but humorous contradictions.

She stared at him, apparently oblivious to her state of undress. "Ignacio says he'll *never* do business with Tarrant Hardcastle."

"I run the estate now." He didn't want to talk about business. Not while his body ached for the feel of her skin against his.

"But isn't he still the legal owner?"

He frowned. A nasty sensation snuck over him, warring with his desire. Had she researched proprietorship of the estate? "Are you afraid you're wasting your time trying to do business with the wrong person?"

"No, of course not. I just…I don't want to cause trouble." Apprehension shone in her dark eyes. She bit her lush lips with those delicate white teeth.

"You don't want to cause trouble?" He let out a harsh laugh. "It's a bit late for that." His life had been so easy once. Before she came. The estate humming smoothly, everyone prosperous and content.

All the family skeletons safely buried in the backyard.

And now? Pain torqued through him in equal measure to the fierce passion that racked his body.

And it was all Susannah's doing.

He stepped toward her, invaded her space. When he brushed his thumb over her chin, her lips parted.

He cocked his head. "You do want our wine, don't you?"

"I do, but…"

"If I want to sell wine to Tarrant Hardcastle, I'll do it. Business is business."

Her telltale wrinkle deepened. He wanted to tell her to stop thinking, but he didn't want to waste breath on arguing, or even talking, so he leaned in to silence her with a kiss.

Relief flashed through him as her lips softened under his, and her mouth opened to welcome his tongue.

Stray thoughts hacked at his consciousness, fighting with

the thick and inviting distraction of lust. *If Ignacio truly considered him his son and rightful heir, he'd not interfere.*

Tension ached in his muscles and he longed to lose himself in her arms. Nothing was certain any more. *If Ignacio no longer saw him as his son and heir, because everyone now knew he was another man's illegitimate son, then let things come to a head.*

His breath grew ragged as he drew Susannah close, wrapping his arms around her slim, lithe body. Her long fingers dug into his back, holding him tight, and the first sweet strains of relief rang through him.

In her passionate embrace, the troubles of the world fell away. Nothing was left but the silky touch of her skin, her sweet breath on his face.

Already, his muscles stung with anticipation of the release they'd share. He nuzzled her neck, and enjoyed her sweet moan.

As his fingers roamed over her back and he buried his face in her hair, his heart ached with fierce longing to forget everything, everyone, except her.

Ten

Susannah lay in Amado's arms, their breathing the only sound in the still air after they made love.

Made love.

Such a common expression. Could you actually bring love into the world by having hot sex? Maybe you could. Something stirred in her heart, painful and difficult to name.

Probably because this was a kind of love that was inappropriate and should never have happened. A passion born of simple lust. The kind of thing she'd been raised to stay away from, and thought herself smart enough to avoid.

A love with no future.

Susannah had a weird sense of being on the edge of a precipice, looking down over the stunning view, admiring it and enjoying its beauty, knowing all the while that at any minute she could plunge into the abyss.

Amado's chest swelled with a deep breath, shifting her weight. "I'll drive you back to the house."

"Okay." Her heart stung at the thought of separating from him. She wanted this magic moment to last a little bit longer.

But she couldn't even protest and say that she wanted to see more of the winemaking operations. Not with any conviction. She'd already proved to both herself and Amado that all thoughts of work and business crumbled in the face of her disturbing hunger for him.

She wasn't even that embarrassed by it. There wasn't anything she could do about it, so what was the point? Would something be gained by denying them both these moments of pleasure? It was too late for them to ever have a crisp business relationship or a casual platonic friendship. If their relationship was going to be messy, then why couldn't it be hot and rough and affectionate, too?

Though, of course it would have been better if they never did any of this in the first place.

Amado's arms closed tightly around her. Squeezed her in an embrace that was almost painful in its intensity. "What's going on in that dangerous brain of yours?"

She hesitated. Was there any harm in telling him the truth? He must surely feel the same way. "I was just wishing that we never slept together."

His eyes narrowed.

"It would have made things so much easier if we never got started, don't you think?"

His muscles tightened. "I dare say."

The air around them seemed to cool. He squeezed out from under her and leaped off the sofa.

Goose bumps rose on her skin, deprived of his warmth.

He grabbed his pants off the floor and shoved them on. "Let's go. I don't want to waste any more of your valuable time."

She eased herself into a sitting position. Wrapped her arms around her suddenly chilled body.

But she didn't regret her honesty. She didn't want to become the kind of person who only told someone what they wanted to hear. "I don't think it's a waste of time. It's beautiful when we…" *make love.* She couldn't bring herself to say it. "It's just that the desire doesn't go away. It comes back stronger each time."

Amado paused in buckling his belt. He stared at her.

"Am I being too frank?"

"No." He frowned, then a gleam of humor entered his eyes. "Yes, maybe. But I like that about you. I'm tired of people who say things they don't mean, so better that you speak the truth." He stepped toward her and cupped her face in his hands. "Even if it might get you into trouble."

A flame of gladness lit in her heart. He understood that she couldn't lie just to make things easier. And she didn't mind being in trouble, at least not this kind.

How crazy was that?

He pressed a hot kiss to her lips, which sent a hot shimmer of arousal surging through her. Maybe she was better off when she didn't know she was capable of these kinds of feelings.

He stepped back and continued dressing. She couldn't help watching. Admiring the muscled lines of his body. Of course she desired him. He was heart-stoppingly handsome, smart, hardworking…

He tucked in his shirt and turned to her. Spoke gruffly. "I'm going to check on our newest Chardonnay vines. You coming?"

He'd asked rather rudely, as if her presence would be an intrusion. But his eyes gleamed with…hope. He was too proud to let her know that he felt—at least a little bit—the same way she did.

Her chest expanded. "I'd *love* to."

Her smart suit was rather crumpled as it had somehow ended up underneath the sofa. Amado didn't seem to notice and luckily there was no one around as they exited the building.

"Where's your car?" She looked around.

"There." A nod of his head indicated a black horse standing tied to a wood fence under a shady arbor. "Don't worry. I'll give you a leg up."

Icy nails of fear raked down her back. "Oh, no. I couldn't. I've never ridden before. And I'm not dressed for it."

He snorted. "The horse doesn't care what you're wearing. I'll lead you. You'll be very comfortable. Estrella is gentle and calm."

Susannah glanced around to see if there would be any other witnesses to her untimely death.

"Seriously, don't be nervous. She's used to carrying guests who can't ride."

"Did you bring her here for me?"

He shrugged. "I thought you should see more of the estate. You haven't explored the vineyards themselves, yet. And I didn't want you to ruin your nice shoes." Humor twinkled in his eyes.

A smile tugged at her mouth. Amado never ceased to surprise her. Even when he'd shown up, curt and brusque, ready to argue with her over labels, he'd fully intended to take her out for a ride to show her his estate. The realization made her heart do a weird little leap.

Okay, now she *had* to get on the horse.

She put her foot in Amado's sturdy hand, and swung her leg over the saddle. She felt awkward perched up in the air.

"What about my car?" she wondered aloud.

"Don't worry about it." Amado looked straight ahead, guiding the horse with its reins in one hand. Although she couldn't see, she could tell he was smiling. "It won't go anywhere."

He turned. "Are you comfortable?"

"Yes." She wasn't entirely lying. As they plodded along the dirt road back toward the house and barn, she started to relax and move with the rolling motion of the horse's back.

She couldn't help enjoying Amado's smile of approval. *How pathetic was this?* Once again it was painfully obvious she'd do anything he asked her to. And he knew it.

He guided the horse over to the side of the road as a car came by. Susannah hoped details of her pony ride wouldn't be broadcast around the estate by dinnertime.

When the car slowed, and the window rolled down, she was surprised to see Clara. "Hello, Amado."

His shoulders stiffened as he murmured a polite greeting.

"I made some of your favorite pastries." Clara glanced at Susannah. "And some for you, too, Susannah. I'm grateful that you came to visit me today."

Amado jerked a glance back at Susannah. She swallowed. "Thank you. I'm sure I'll enjoy them."

Clara glanced at how Amado was leading Susannah on the horse, and a mysterious smile came over her face. "I can see you're both busy so I'll leave them at the house for you."

"Fine." Amado remained rigid as Clara drove away.

Susannah couldn't stop a satisfied smile from appearing. It cheered her to see Clara venture back to Amado's domain. "I think she's calming down a bit. If only your dad would…"

"I don't want to talk about them." He turned sharply off

the road and led the horse right through what looked like a vegetable garden, then a rather rough pasture, and up into the rows of vines.

Susannah stayed quiet as Amado marched along the rows, the horse's head at his shoulder. Lush green shoots and leaves reminded her it was summer down here, even as everything was busy freezing solid in New York.

"You're looking more relaxed up there. Want to take the reins? She won't go anywhere."

She shook her head. "You must think I'm ridiculous. I suppose you were galloping around when you were three."

He smiled. "I was. But everyone's different and I don't want to push you. Let me help you down."

He held the horse while she slid ungracefully off it. Then, bending at the waist, he examined the dusty green leaves of a young grape vine. He held the leaf between his thumb and finger, tender and careful as he was...with her.

She could tell he'd be a great father himself, one day. Encouraging his children to explore and to follow their dreams, and supporting them when they didn't have the strength to do it all on their own.

She realized she'd let out an audible sigh, because Amado turned to look at her. She tried to cover up. "It's so beautiful here. I can see why you never want to travel."

"On a purely practical level, it's an excellent *terroir*." He lifted a brow.

"It is." The *terroir*—or the specific vineyard location including climate, soil, altitude and sun exposure—was what gave each wine its unique character and flavor. "And you've found a way to capture the magic of this place in your wines. You're lucky that Ignacio gave you free rein to experiment and to put the land to your own uses."

He frowned. "He's lucky I chose to. The land had been

overgrazed. You can't follow tradition forever and hope for the best." His jaw set in a hard line.

"You're so angry with him. He loves you and he just wanted the best for you."

"How do you know? Is that why he drove away my Valentina?"

Susannah's heart clenched at this mention of the mysterious Valentina. She remembered the name from his angry confrontation with Ignacio.

Obviously Valentina meant more to Amado than any other woman. "Was she your fiancée?"

He stared at the rocky horizon. "A long time ago." He turned to look at her. "She taught me to dance. And a lot of other things I didn't know before. We wanted to marry but Ignacio forbade it. He said she was *unsuitable*."

Disgust darkened his voice. "Yes, her family wasn't rich. She was born out of wedlock and her mother raised her alone. But who cares? As you said, that kind of thing doesn't matter anymore. I wasn't looking for a rich wife to support me." He blew out a disgusted breath. "Now that I know more, I think they refused to let me marry at that time because they didn't want someone to go hunting for my birth certificate and find out I wasn't who they said I was."

A chill trickled down Susannah's spine. "So, Ignacio made her leave?"

"I wanted us to leave together. To move somewhere else and make a new start." He looked over the vines, growing lush with new leaves. "She wouldn't hear of me leaving Tierra de Oro. She wouldn't let me because she knew how much this place meant to me. So one night, she went away. She had no family here, no one at all, except me. I tried to follow her, but she turned me away. Told me to go home, where I belonged."

She could hear the emotion in his voice, fresh as if it had happened yesterday.

"I'm so sorry."

"Ignacio should be sorry. Valentina and I loved each other, but that meant nothing to him. All he cared about was keeping his stupid secret. Preserving the family honor." He snorted. "What kind of honor is it that chooses lies over the truth?"

"Do you think he forced her to leave?"

Amado nodded slowly. "Once she was gone and the crisis was over, they must have realized this would always be a problem, so they had someone forge a new birth certificate. I have a copy of it at the house, listing Ignacio and Clara as my father and mother. It's one of the reasons I didn't believe your crazy story when you first showed up here."

"Wow."

"See? The deception goes deep. For the last ten years, they've been begging me to marry. To continue the legacy." Fresh pain glittered in his dark eyes. "A legacy of deception. Maybe I should have left here long ago to stay with the woman I loved. But Ignacio deprived me of even that choice."

His face was taut with emotion. In spite of herself, she couldn't help wishing he had the same strong feelings for her.

Ridiculous! They were both adults. Older, wiser and far too sensible for a grand passion.

Weren't they? So why did a powerful sensation unfold inside her every time he looked at her?

"And you haven't been in love since?" The moment the question left her lips, she cursed herself. What business was it of hers to pry into his love life?

"No."

His curt answer cut deep. *Of course he doesn't love you! Stop fishing for compliments. Or whatever it is you're doing.*

She forced a casual laugh. "I guess you just keep your-self busy having affairs with foreign visitors."

Amado's eyes narrowed. "Yes."

His answer fell like a crushing blow to the chest. She'd done it again. Asked a question hoping for a specific answer, and had it come back to smack her down instead.

She managed to keep her composure despite the ache of sadness creeping over her. "The buds are forming."

Amado took one of the tight furls between his thumb and finger. "Yes, this will be their first year in production."

"Soon they'll be ready to make more liquid gold from Tierra de Oro." She forced a casual smile.

Amado shot her a crooked smile. "We should work that into our PR."

"I suspect Hardcastle Enterprises can help you with that." Phew. Back to business. Much better than talking about who Amado did or didn't love.

But funny how she just spoke about her employer in the third person. She would normally have said "we" will help you.

Her stomach tightened at the prospect of Tarrant Hard-castle getting his fingers in Amado's carefully tended family business. He was Amado's biological father, but still...

"How do you feel about selling your wines through Hardcastle?"

He stroked the horse's neck. "I like it. I'm ready for change. I think it's time to take Tierra De Oro to the next level."

She nodded. Shoved down the rush of misgivings that rose through her. "Great."

* * *

Back at the house, she picked up the phone and called New York. Amado was keen to do business with Hardcastle, and it was her job to make it happen, regardless of her personal feelings. She managed to describe her progress in convincing Amado to update the *bodega*'s image.

"Marvelous!" Tarrant's exuberance reverberated down the phone line. "I'll have Dino come up with some sketches. Perhaps we can have them printed by next week. Make sure none of their old labels go on any more bottles."

Susannah winced. All she'd done was sketch the idea verbally, and Tarrant was ready to take it to the presses.

But that's how things worked at Hardcastle Enterprises. No doubt why he'd been so successful, too. No time wasted pussyfooting around and trying to make everyone else happy, when only one person counted: Tarrant.

She cleared her throat. "So, how many cases do you want me to bring over? Last year they produced about four thousand, and this year should be more, as long as the harvest goes well."

Silence. "Buy them all."

"What?"

"All. Every case. Every single bottle. And no fussing about consignments and percentages. We'll buy them outright at the price he agrees to."

Susannah's mouth dropped open. Tarrant wanted Amado to write his own ticket.

But he also wanted him to be completely in Hardcastle Enterprises' pocket.

"He has existing customers. An established distribution network here in South America."

And a father—or grandfather—who hates your guts.

What would happen if this sparked a head-to-head confrontation between Amado and Ignacio over control of the estate?

A dismissive snort echoed through the earpiece. "We'll put Tierra de Oro vineyard on the map. Next year he'll be able to charge double or triple for each bottle. Tierra de Oro will be minting money and I don't think he'll have any complaints."

Susannah winced. She could see Tarrant's perspective. No doubt he liked the idea of being the benevolent father he hadn't bothered to be earlier.

As a business arrangement though, it was patronizing and she wasn't even sure Amado would agree. He was clearly proud of the customer base he'd developed over the last decade. He'd traveled around, handselling the wine, case by case, to restaurants and hotels, building warm personal relationships with many of his customers. The stories he'd told her had made her fall even more in love with him.

Her thoughts screeched to a halt.

She was *not* in love with him. It was one thing to have that thought during the bedazzlement of lovemaking, quite another to have it in the scorching light of day. Especially since he'd come right out and affirmed that she was just another tourist, to him.

Her heart squeezed.

"Susannah? You still there?"

"Um, okay. I'll talk to him."

"Based on your impressive performance so far, I'm sure you'll convince him."

Eleven

Susannah felt like a sneak for going behind Amado's back. She even crept through the vegetable gardens and around the pastures, to avoid being seen on the road.

Amado might not care about her, but she cared about him. She also cared about Tierra de Oro and the people who worked there. She couldn't risk encouraging Amado into a deal that might somehow destroy the whole vineyard.

Ignacio was behind their steel-and-glass house, pruning geraniums in some clay pots on the patio. Clara spotted her through a window and waved.

A rush of relief rose through Susannah as she saw them together in the same space. Well, almost. Hopefully their relationship was on the road to repair.

Ignacio was a big man, stocky and well-built. Dressed in a finely checked shirt with khaki pants and leather boots, he looked every bit the gentleman rancher he was.

She moved as close as she dared and cleared her throat. He swung around and saw her.

Her heart pounded beneath her dress as she cleared her throat. "I know you don't want me here. In a lot of ways I wish I could turn the clock back to before my first trip and change everything back to the way it was."

She swallowed, aware of a painful truth. She wouldn't willingly give up her precious time with Amado for anything.

Ignacio grunted, still snipping away at a plant.

"But I can't. I came as an employee, doing a job that I enjoy very much, bringing great wines to people's tables. I'm here *today* because I, Susannah Clarke, take personal responsibility in what I do." Her hands trembled. She wasn't going to hide behind the shimmering steel barricades of Hardcastle Enterprises anymore. Something in her tone of voice made Ignacio look up.

She held his gaze. "My employer, Tarrant Hardcastle, would like to buy all of this year's wine from Tierra de Oro."

Ignacio put down his shears and rose to his full height. His mouth tightened into a flat line, but the look in his eyes made her chest constrict.

"It would be a financial boon for the vineyard, as he has instructed me to let Amado set his own price." She held her head high, wanting to let him know that she wasn't trying to cheat them.

"*All* the wine? I've never heard of such a thing."

"He has deep pockets."

"He wants to control my son." His jaw stiffened. "*His* son."

She couldn't argue. Tarrant was not above trying to buy affection, or coerce it, if necessary.

"If Amado does this…" He shook his head. Strong emotion traversed the weathered planes of his face. He pressed a fist to his heart.

Susannah inhaled a shaky breath. "I feel strange asking this. Totally out of place, in fact, but does Amado even have the right to do this?"

He paused. Stared at her, his blue eyes distant. "Do you mean, is it his vineyard, or mine?"

She nodded.

He rubbed a hand over his face. "Legally, of course, on paper, it's still mine and has been since my father died and left it to me." His broad chest rose as he inhaled deeply. "But the *bodega* and all its wine are truly Amado's. If not on paper, then here." He tapped his chest with his fist.

"He brought the vineyard to life, figured out how to finance the winery, chased down the customers, encouraged the tourists. He grew it from the seed of his imagination into what you see today."

Sorrow flickered in his eyes as he looked at her. "I'm proud of him for his accomplishments and I would never try to take that away from him. In that sense, yes, he has every right to do with *his* wine as *he* wishes."

Susannah heaved a sigh of relief. At least this deal-with-the-devil wouldn't result in Amado getting kicked off the estate. She couldn't have lived with herself if she'd been a part of that.

But that wasn't the end of it. She also couldn't live with herself if the deal caused a permanent rift in the family. She cleared her throat. "Um, how do you feel about the idea?"

He paused for a moment, eyes wide. Then he let out a coarse burst of laughter that made her take a step back. "How do I feel?" His chest heaved. "What kind of pop psychology question is that? How do I feel that my son chooses to hand over his life's work to the son-of-a-bitch

who gave him life by accident, and turn his back on the
man who raised him?"

Red-faced and still pounding his fist to his chest, the
older man looked like he was about to have a heart attack.
"But to answer your carefully put question, no, I won't
assert my right to control the vineyard and cast him out.
Even if he no longer considers me his father, I will *always*
consider Amado to be my son."

The door opened and Clara stepped out onto the patio.

Tears shone in Ignacio's eyes as he stared at Susannah.
She had a feeling he'd just arrived at this revelation himself. His anger and resentment at the situation had crys-
tallized down to its core—his deep and enduring love for
Amado.

Clara laid a hand on his sleeve. He took her hand and
held it in his. "Amado was a gift to me. He arrived unex-
pectedly, and as the result of a tragedy, but he brought joy
I could never have imagined. And he brought me my beautiful and wonderful wife, Clara."

Ignacio bent his head and kissed her hand. Two fat tears
rolled down Clara's cheeks, which flushed pink. He
brushed one away with a leathery thumb. "She married an
angry widower who'd lost his child. Her demanding boss,
no less. What kind of person takes a chance like that?"

He shook his head, staring at her in wonder. "Her kind
and selfless gift—of her own life—transformed a disaster
into the sweetest joy a man can experience in his lifetime."
He pressed his hands to her cheeks and kissed her. Clara
blinked, her ample chest heaving with unsteady breaths.

Susannah's stomach trembled at the raw display of
emotion and affection by these two reserved people. She
found herself backing away, unworthy to witness this
profound moment in their lives.

Maybe one day she'd be worthy of such deep affection.

She cursed herself for her foolish, selfish thought. "Thank you," she managed. "I'll be going now."

Susannah walked slowly back across the property to the house. Theoretically, everything could work out fine. Amado would make a deal with Tarrant, the value of his wines would rise, he'd make lots of money, Ignacio would be prickly at first but eventually get used to the idea and…

She couldn't do it.

Once Hardcastle Enterprises got their fingers into Tierra de Oro, it would change forever. They wouldn't even mean to change it, but they would. Demands for increased production, greater efficiency, cost reduction.

Once Amado kissed-off his old customers, he'd become dependent on Hardcastle. Subject to the whims of a director in a boardroom, just as she was herself.

Tierra de Oro was more than a vineyard. As Ignacio had acknowledged, it was Amado's whole life, planned and planted and cherished into lush fruition. This new alliance—even if it was with his own blood—could stunt and warp the growth and change everything.

And she didn't want any part of that. Even if it meant quitting the job she loved.

She turned to look up at the mountains and pulled her phone from her pocket.

"What do you mean you *can't* do it?" Tarrant's voice rose over the phone. "My son doesn't want to sell his wines to me?" His voice was tight.

"He does. But *I* don't think he should. I don't think it's in the best interests of the estate. They have a diverse client base and deep roots in the community." Her voice shook.

"And who are you to have an opinion?" Anger and arrogance colored his voice.

"I may not be important, but I set this in motion, and I feel responsible. I won't be a party to it." She swallowed hard. *Here goes nothing.* "I'd like to offer my resignation."

"Accepted."

Susannah tracked Amado down in one of the vineyards near the house. She saw him first, and she couldn't help pausing for a moment. He looked so handsome, the tanned skin of his cheeks warmed by the late afternoon sun, hair and shirt collar tossing in the breeze.

She'd miss him very much. Now she no longer worked for Hardcastle, she'd have no reason to come back here. Ever.

"Amado."

He turned, and a quick smile lit his face.

Her heart thundered against her ribs as she picked her way along a row of vines and he walked toward her at the same time.

A romantic image, but there was no romance here. He'd have every reason to hate her for going against his wishes. For angering his newfound father.

She'd tried to find a smooth path. An easy way out. But sometimes there just wasn't one, no matter how hard you looked for it. Maybe she'd hoped her former boss would beg her to stay. That he'd ask her to come up with an equitable compromise that would benefit both Hardcastle Enterprises and the vineyard.

But he hadn't.

She stopped a few feet from him and blurted out the truth. "Tarrant wants to buy your entire output."

Amado stopped walking. It was late in the day and the sun hung low in the sky, at the high mountain peaks. He narrowed his eyes against the harsh afternoon light. "Why?"

She looked straight at him. "I suppose he wants to support you, or to own you. Or something in between. Maybe it's his warped way of showing he cares."

His frown deepened. "The price?"

"He said you should set it." She straightened her shoulders. "I told him I wouldn't be any part of it."

"Why?" The word exploded from his mouth.

"I don't think it's a good idea, for the estate, or for you."

"It's not a good idea to set our own price for wine that will find its way onto the tables of connoisseurs in the U.S. who will raise the value of our brand?" He blew out an angry breath. "Do you think our wines aren't ready? That they're not superior enough?"

"I think your wines could go anywhere, and I'm confident that they will. But I don't think you should let Hardcastle Enterprises take over your distribution. It's a tightly run business, with concrete and aggressive business goals. Soon, they'd make demands that you might not want to meet."

"Or that *you* don't think we could meet."

"I don't have any investment either way. I quit my job." The words drifted out of her mouth and hung in the air.

"You *what?*"

"I've done enough damage here in my role as a representative of Hardcastle Enterprises. Yes, I loved my work, but I couldn't look myself in the mirror if I encouraged you to take this offer, and I couldn't take my paycheck if I didn't."

He stared at her, angry and accusatory. Even then her body responded, chest swelling and nipples tightening.

It didn't matter. Soon she'd be gone and her body would return to its normal state.

Pain pierced her heart at the prospect of leaving for

good. But she had no choice. At least she'd leave with her conscience intact, and at the end of the day, she'd found that's what mattered to her most.

Amado's stern gaze had drifted lower over the simple dress she'd chosen for travel.

She tried to ignore the way her skin heated. She couldn't control her physical reaction to him. She'd learned to accept that. She was only human.

The silence between them finally forced words to her tongue. "Selling the estate's output to Tarrant would hurt your father terribly. I know you're angry with him now for what he did to Valentina, but do you really want to drive a permanent wedge between you? You all live here and love this place, and it's better to embrace the future as a family."

Amado's jaw stiffened. "As you forced me to learn, Tarrant Hardcastle is my father."

"In a purely technical sense, yes."

"And you've decided—in your infinite wisdom—that's how it should remain."

"I think it would be good for you to grow closer to Tarrant, but not at the expense of Tierra de Oro, or your relationship with Ignacio."

"You know everything, don't you?"

His hard stare threw down a challenge and she shivered under its force. "I thought I knew a lot more than I did. I thought I could do my job and make my boss happy then get back to doing the work I enjoy."

She drew in a shaky breath. "I can't. You can speak to Tarrant directly and make any kind of deal you want, but I won't be a party to it."

He tipped his head. Pale gold sunlight played off the planes of his high cheekbones. "So easy to wash your hands of us, is it? No doubt you're ready to continue your travels. To visit somewhere with less emotional drama to deal with."

He took a step toward her. "Somewhere you have more distance. More control."

Her belly contracted as he stepped into her personal space. His scent assaulted her, brashly male, soap and skin and sweat from a long day.

She blinked, trying to fight off a rush of feelings. "I don't want to harm the growing relationship between you and Tarrant. But I don't want to destroy your relationship with Ignacio either."

"It's always about someone else, isn't it? It's never about *you*."

She faltered. "I've just been a messenger here. A facilitator. But I can't play that role anymore, so I'm leaving."

"Huh. Like your parents. Bringing the word of God—or Tarrant Hardcastle in this case—to change the lives of everyone around them. Then they pack their bags and move on."

Susannah stood speechless. "This has nothing to do with my parents."

"No? I think you learned to live as a permanent tourist. Always on the outside, looking in. Offering advice and keeping a scientific distance."

He took one step closer. She could feel his body heat, almost hear his pulse in the air. Her own heartbeat raced and thundered.

"Until you met me." He seized her around the waist and pressed his lips to hers, hard, hot and unrelenting. She tried to push back, to regain control, but her legs buckled and suddenly her arms were around his strong back, clinging to him.

Emotion flooded through her, devastating in its intensity. Even as she kissed him back with force, she couldn't help hating him for this last show of the humiliating power he had over her.

He pulled back as fast as he'd started. Stepped away. Left her shivering and tingling and gasping for breath. "It's just sex isn't it? Simple lust." Eyes narrowed and mouth savage, he stood a couple of feet from her.

She nodded.

"I'm sure you can analyze it out of existence if you try hard enough. Leaving is a good start."

He stared at her. Daring her to just turn and go. To put him and Tierra de Oro behind her and get on with her life. To go where she felt safe, protected from the emotional storms she'd helped unleash and which had now buffeted her own life right off course.

He looked at her feet. Perhaps waiting for them to move. To start walking along the brick walkway to the house. Someone, possibly Amado, had driven her car back to the house from the vineyard. Her bag was already in the trunk.

But as his eyes rested on her feet—low-heeled ballet flats now covered with sandy dust—she couldn't help but remember that foot massage he'd given her on her first night. She was a stranger, an obnoxious and rather arrogant one from a foreign country, with a crazy tale that insulted his family, and he'd taken the time to help her relax and feel at home. In his bed.

Emotion welled up and spilled out into words. "It's your fault too. I didn't ask to be seduced. I've never slept with anyone, ever, on any of my business trips. You started it!" Her playground-style accusation rang in the air.

"Of course. I led you astray. I apologize." His dark eyes glittered.

"I thought it would be fun," she blathered on. "I didn't realize…" She paused and swallowed hard.

"Didn't realize what? That you're a woman, capable of feelings?"

Her breathing was audible and she could barely control it. She blinked as the sun slipped behind the barn roof and sent a sharp ray directly into her line of vision. "Yes," she whispered.

Feelings. That simple word really didn't describe the disturbing and confusing array of sensations and emotions that bedeviled her whenever she even thought of Amado.

Why couldn't they say goodbye nicely? Why did he have to be so hostile? She'd simply done what she was asked to do. She hadn't meant to hurt anyone.

Her chest constricted. "I'll never forget our time together." Unable to stand there a moment longer without bursting into angry and ashamed sobs, she turned and ran along the brick path, blinded by hot tears.

Amado stared after Susannah as she ran. Anger surged through him. She could just run away and leave? In a few hours, she'd be on a plane. Back in the States. Getting on with her life.

I'll never forget our time together.

A shocked laugh fled his lips. He was just another snapshot in her mental photo album. She dismissed their deep connection as just another of his "affairs with foreign visitors."

He'd brought her here to get her out of his system. To slake the crazy lust she aroused in him. He'd planned to enjoy her until he grew tired of her charms, then send her on her way.

And now she was leaving because she didn't want to *deal* anymore? She'd quit the job she loved to get away from him?

"Hey, fool, why aren't you running after her?"

He spun around to see Rosa standing on the path, a bowl of fresh eggs in her hands.

"Run after her? What for? She's dying to get away."

"Maybe she thinks she is, but you know better."

"What are you talking about, you crazy old woman?"

She walked toward him, looked right at him with those penetrating dark eyes that could read his mind since he was a barefoot brat.

"She loves you." She said it quietly. The words rested in the air between them for a few seconds.

"No, she doesn't. She's leaving of her own free will."

"Just like Valentina left of her own free will all those years ago?" She shook her head. "You could have gone away with her, but you didn't because you knew that your place was at Tierra de Oro."

"She turned me away."

"She did it because she loved you and she wanted to keep your family together."

Her words cut deep. The truth hurt. "Ignacio drove her away."

"And now you're going to let him do the same thing again? I've worked for this family since I was a girl and Ignacio's always been too stubborn and pigheaded for his own good. He loved Clara for ten agonizing years before you finally came along and brought them together in a so-called 'business arrangement'. It was pathetic the way the two of them pussyfooted around each other, pretending they didn't love each other for all those years. If you hadn't come along, they'd probably still be moping about and sleeping alone."

She blew out an exasperated snort. "I'm too old to watch another Alvarez push away the woman he loves because of his stupid pride. Run after her!" She gestured with a gnarled hand.

Amado couldn't help turning to look down the path. Susannah was already out of sight. A fierce pang of loss kicked him in the gut. "She doesn't love me."

His words came out low and kind of choked. Humiliating. He couldn't even believe he was arguing with his ninety-something former nursemaid over this.

"She does, and she's showed her love by trying to save your family, even if it means leaving here for good."

He frowned, squinting in the sun. How did Rosa always know everything?

She raised a hand in the air. "And you love her too, even if you're too thick-skulled to realize it right now. Now, get out of my way before these eggs turn sour. Shoo!"

A rough volley of barking propelled him along the path back to the house. He jogged, but didn't run. He wasn't going to chase after another woman who could walk out of his life without a backward glance.

But when he saw the scene in front of the house, he broke into a sprint. Cástor and Pólux had Susannah pinned to the gravel beside her rented car.

"Help!" Her voice rose through the gruff barks.

Cástor leaned over to lick her face. Amado stopped running. A smile crept across his face. "They're not hurting you." The dogs seemed to be lavishing her with affection.

"They don't know their own strength. And one of them is standing on my dress so I can't get up."

Pólux had planted himself neatly over her legs, pinning her on both sides and in the middle by standing on the skirt of her floaty dress. His dogs turned to look up at him with their mournful, doting stares.

Did we do good, Daddy?

He couldn't keep a raw burst of laughter from leaving his mouth. "I don't think they want to let you leave." He summoned the dogs off her and offered his hand.

She took it. As he pulled her to her feet he noticed her face was streaked with tears.

His stomach coiled into a knot. "What happened? Are you okay? My dogs don't usually act like this."

"I just wanted to pet them goodbye. Give them a hug." She inhaled shakily. "And they got carried away and knocked me over."

"They're affectionate dogs."

"I know." She blinked and two fresh tears rolled down her cheeks. "I still remember their enthusiastic greeting on my first visit. I'll miss them."

The rift of loss in Amado's gut opened into a chasm.

You can't leave.

Could Rosa be right? He frowned, trying to gather his thoughts. He tended to get overwhelmed by emotion and sensation around Susannah and he couldn't think straight.

Was that love? It felt more like madness.

Susannah looked right at him, her eyelashes glittering with tears. "I'll miss you very much."

Her raw, personal confession kicked him where it hurt. Right now he couldn't imagine life without her. He wanted to take her to his bed. Not even for sex. Just to hold her.

"Why do you have to leave?" The words departed his mouth before he had a chance to stop them. They came out gruff and demanding.

"I've caused enough trouble. I thought I was helping, but I'm not. I've made a mess and I don't know how to fix it." Her shoulders shook as a sob racked her. "I got personally involved when I shouldn't have."

"Who says you shouldn't have?" He took a step toward her. Fought the urge to bury his hand in her loose dark hair.

"You." She lifted her chin.

He stopped. He had told her to stay out of his business. To leave Clara and Ignacio alone. Her meddling attempts to repair his broken family suddenly touched him.

"And you're right," she continued, head held high. "I don't want to tell you what to do with your vineyard. I especially don't want to tell you to do something that I don't think is right."

"I value your advice."

"I know." That familiar little groove appeared next to her brow. "You've taken my unwanted advice with such good grace. Treated me with respect and offered me your hospitality. It was all okay as long as I was just doing my job, representing my boss." She paused and he watched her chest rise and fall inside her delicate dress.

Longing mingled with desire choked him.

"But you're right. I can't go through life being someone else's representative. I have to do what I, Susannah Clarke, think is right."

"Even if it means giving up the job you love."

She blinked, tears still fresh in her eyes. "Yes. Tierra de Oro is a special place, and I couldn't live with a clear conscience if I did anything to hurt the estate or the people who love it."

"Because you also love Tierra de Oro."

She bit her lip, that thoughtful line still deep. "Yes, if you can love a place on such short acquaintance."

He could see her attempting to analyze and understand. Her busy mind trying so hard to tackle something that could never be understood, only felt. The urge to hold her, to simply take her in his arms, was almost unbearable. "Some people say you can fall in love at first sight."

"That's not love. That's attraction." She tilted her head. "But it invites you to explore. To seek out the spirit of a place. Or to wait for it to reveal itself to you. That doesn't take long."

"Maybe only a single day."

"Or one night." The tears appeared again.

They weren't talking about just a place, anymore.

I'm too old to watch another Alvarez push away the woman he loves because of his stupid pride. Rosa's words buzzed in his confused brain, tangled with the thoughts and feelings gathering there.

Ever since Susannah had come to Tierra de Oro on her difficult errand, he'd been unable to get her out of his mind. When she wasn't around, he missed the light that sparkled in her dark eyes. He hungered for her thoughtful opinions and craved the touch of her gentle hands.

"Susannah." He stepped forward and picked up her hand, which trembled in his. "You coming here awakened something in me. Something good and something bad." He frowned, trying to organize his thoughts. "Bad because I learned I'd been lied to by the people I loved most. But good, because in testing those relationships I realized how much I have to lose."

His heart ached almost to bursting as he struggled to put his feelings into words. "I think the worst thing that could happen, Susannah—" he squeezed her hand, too hard probably, as adrenaline spiked through him "—would be to lose you."

She stared at him, blinking. Confusion fluttered across her always-composed face.

"What I'm trying to say is…" He dragged in a breath. "Is that I love you."

The words reverberated in the air, and seemed to bounce off the old stucco facing of his familiar home, off the gravel of the road and the sharp blue sky.

"I love you, too."

Her reply startled him. He was still wrapped up in his own pronouncement. In how true it felt and what a huge relief it was to get the confession off his chest.

"You do?"

Tears sparkled in her eyes even as a smile tugged at her mouth. "Yes. I think I loved you since that first night here, when I realized it was going to be harder than I thought to just walk away."

"Don't walk away. Stay here with me."

She frowned, emotion tugging at her delicate features.

"I know it's a different country, but you've traveled and lived in many places. You'll help me run the vineyard, and market our wines, and anything else you want to do." His heart soared as the vision unfurled in his mind.

Susannah's entire expression had gone blank. Even that tricky and revealing wrinkle he loved so much had disappeared. "Me? Here?"

"Why not?" He pulled her to him, grasped both her hands in both of his.

"But I don't have any experience." Sadness shadowed her eyes.

"With what? Staying in one place? It's easy. You just don't go anywhere."

"I mean with fitting in. Being part of a community. Look at me!" She gestured at her dress. A very lovely yellow, decorated with dusty paw marks. "I'm visiting a farm and I wore a dress."

He grinned. "I *love* your dresses. In case you haven't noticed, Clara and Rosa always wear skirts, too. I guess it's an Alvarez family tradition. See? You already fit right in."

"Do you think?" Her shy glance stabbed him in the heart.

"I know it." Unable to control himself any longer, he pulled her into his arms and kissed her with every ounce of passion and energy he possessed.

When he paused for breath, he managed to rasp, "Will you marry me, Susannah? Will you be my wife?"

Her lips parted. "Oh, goodness." She searched his face. "Do you think I could? Even after what I did?"

His heart clenched. How could she still feel guilty for just doing what she had to? "I'll always be grateful you took on the unenviable task of bringing me the news about my parentage."

Her eyes widened. "You will?"

"Yes, because now I know who I am. Not who everyone wants me to be or expects me to be. I'm glad the cobwebs of lies and secrets have been blown out of Tierra de Oro and bright new sunlight can pour in. I'm glad I met my biological father before it's too late." He rubbed her hands, enjoying the warmth he found there. "I found a new piece of me and at the same time I found you." He hesitated. Drew in a shaky breath. "Please say you'll marry me."

Tears sparkled in her eyes. "I'd love to marry you and be your wife." She let out something between a laugh and a sob. "Will you be my husband?"

Only Susannah would feel the need to invite him into her life as well. And why not? Her quiet strength and resolution captivated him. Since she arrived he'd been annoyed and entranced in equal measure as she swept house in his life and heart. She'd turned the family upside down and shaken loose emotion they'd kept bottled up for years. No doubt she'd keep them on their toes in the future, too. He couldn't wait to savor every minute of it.

"It would be my great honor and joy to be your husband."

She smiled, pulled him close and kissed him full on the mouth. Exhilaration swept through him like a spring wind and he couldn't help laughing with joy.

Spending the rest of his life with Susannah promised to be a wonderful adventure.

Epilogue

"Goodness, what's that?" Samantha Hardcastle grabbed Susannah's arm. They stared at what looked like an entire cow strapped to a vast wrought-iron gate and suspended over an open firepit.

Susannah laughed. She was still getting used to the local customs herself. "Mendocinos take their *parilla* very seriously."

"What's *parilla?*"

"I'm sorry! I'm forgetting how to speak English already. It's barbecue, which is a real art form here. Ignacio raised the meat himself."

The rich aroma of almost-roasted beef was intoxicating. Sparks from the fire crackled and spat, echoing the excitement in the air. The garden glowed with the last rays of sunset, and lanterns shone in the trees and around the tables decorated for their wedding feast.

Sam leaned in to her and whispered. "Look at Ignacio and Tarrant."

The two *padres familias* stood squared off, their arms raised wide as if to say, "it was this big!"

"Men!" exclaimed Sam. "They don't change much, I'm afraid. I learned that somewhere between my second and third marriages. You just have to love them as they are."

Susannah couldn't help a shy smile sneaking across her face. "I'm looking forward to it."

"You're so lucky, you and Amado, having so many glorious years to look forward to. Do say you'll make me a grandma soon."

Susannah's heart clenched as she saw tears glisten in Sam's eyes. Poor Sam was barely thirty and no doubt wanted a child herself, but that wouldn't be possible with Tarrant so ill. Soon her third marriage would end too and leave her a widow, yet she managed to smile and be happy for two newlyweds with their whole lives ahead of them.

Susannah couldn't help putting her arms around the woman whose spirit shone so brightly despite her troubles. "You're welcome here any time you like, you know. With Tarrant or just by yourself. Think of Tierra de Oro as your second home in Argentina." Then she laughed. "Or is it your twelfth home? I suppose you have a few already."

Sam smiled. "Tarrant always did love to travel. The doctors told him not to come here under any circumstances, but he said he'd rather be dead than miss his son's wedding. Goodness, look at them now!"

Susannah turned to see Tarrant and Ignacio locked in a bear hug.

"What have you ladies done to my fathers?" Amado's deep voice crept into Susannah's ear as he stepped between her and Sam and slid his strong arms around their waists.

"I bet it was that speech Sam gave about how you can't change the past but you can change the future. They look like they're ready to weep and they haven't even tasted our steak yet."

"I think the wedding left everyone a little emotional," Susannah whispered. She brushed a lock of hair from her new husband's forehead. He looked breathtakingly handsome in his dark suit and white shirt. "I know I am, even after my mother gave us that sobering lecture about the duties of a wife to her spouse."

Amado smiled his familiar crooked smile and laid a soft kiss on her cheek. "I'm going to hold you to those, *querida*. Especially the part about how you support the sacred institution of marriage when you keep your husband happy in bed." His hushed tones sent a shiver of giggly excitement through her. Amado laughed. "I guess missionary work has changed a bit since I was in school."

She shrugged, smiling. "They're unusual people."

"Just like their daughter." He looked at Sam. "Is she the most beautiful woman on the planet, or am I just crazily in love with her?"

He stepped back and Susannah blushed under his admiring gaze.

"It's this lovely dress." She smoothed the cleverly cut white silk that molded to her slim body and found curves where she never knew she had them. "Rosa and Clara made it themselves. Aren't they brilliant?"

Sam's eyes widened. "Goodness, yes. They'd give Vera Wang designs a run for the money."

"They said they used to make all their own clothes when they were younger. Can you imagine?"

"No, way." Sam laughed. "The fashion industry might fall apart if I started doing that."

It was a Hardcastle Enterprises joke that Sam dressed only in couture originals. At least Susannah used to think it was a joke. Now she was a family insider, she knew better. Apparently designers even came to their Upper East Side mansion for fittings at Tarrant's insistence.

Susannah couldn't imagine how Sam put up with her ebullient husband, but it was obvious she loved him desperately. What would her life be like when he was gone?

As if he was thinking the same thing, Amado wrapped his arm around Sam's shoulders. "You're my third mom, you know? I think Marisa would be so happy to see us all here together." He rubbed her arm. "It's all your doing, Sam. You started the search for Tarrant's lost children."

Tears welled in Susannah's eyes as she watched the emotion flickering on Sam's face.

Sam dabbed at her eye makeup with a designer handkerchief. "Thank you, Amado. I can't put into words how much it means to me to see you all together, and so happy. This wedding is a wonderful blessing. Tarrant keeps outliving his doctors' expectations and it's because his children are giving him such joyous events to look forward to."

Her carefully made-up lips quivered. "Maybe he really will live a long and full life, just to spite them all." She laughed through sudden tears, and Amado squeezed her hand.

"This evening will live forever in all our hearts," he said softly. "Would you do us the honor of ringing the bell to call everyone to eat?"

"I'd be thrilled."

As the sound of the old brass bell reverberated off the stone buildings, guests made their way into the lovely garden. Ignacio with his arm affectionately wrapped around his beloved Clara, Tarrant helped by his daughter Fiona, Dominic and his wife Bella already practicing their tango steps, Susannah's own parents speaking in animated Spanish to Tomás. Susannah had even found Valentina, who traveled from the *Pampas* with her husband and three children to join the celebration.

The newly united families joined with friends, neighbors and vineyard workers to share slow-roasted steaks, homegrown vegetables and fresh ice cream. Dinner stretched into a long, sweaty, breathless night of dancing, and Amado and Susannah's wedding was celebrated with toasts and tears and many, many glasses of the very best wine on earth.

* * * * *

Eight years ago Matt Shaffer had vanished out of Natalie Rothchild's life, leaving behind a one-line note tucked under a pillow that had grown cold: *I'm sorry, but this just isn't going to work.*

That was it. No explanation, no real indication of remorse. The note had been as clinical and compassionless as an eviction notice, which, in effect, it had been, Natalie thought as she navigated through the morning traffic. Matt had written the note to evict her from his life.

She'd spent the next two weeks crying, breaking down without warning as she walked down the street, or as she sat staring at a meal she couldn't bring herself to eat.

Candace, she remembered with a bittersweet pang, had tried to get her to go clubbing in order to get her to forget about Matt.

She'd turned her twin down, but she did get her act

together. If Matt didn't think enough of their relationship to try to contact her, to try to make her understand why he'd changed so radically from lover to stranger, then to hell with him. He was dead to her, she resolved. And he'd remained that way.

Until twenty minutes ago.

The adrenaline in her veins kept mounting.

Natalie focused on her driving. Vegas in the daylight wasn't nearly as alluring, as magical and glitzy as it was after dark. Like an aging woman best seen in soft lighting, Vegas's imperfections were all visible in the daylight. Natalie supposed that was why people like her sister didn't like to get up until noon. They lived for the night.

Except that Candace could no longer do that.

The thought brought a fresh, sharp ache with it.

"Damn it, Candy, what a waste," Natalie murmured under her breath.

She pulled up before the Janus casino. One of the three valets currently on duty came to life and made a beeline for her vehicle.

"Welcome to the Janus," the young attendant said cheerfully as he opened her door with a flourish.

"We'll see," she replied solemnly.

As he pulled away with her car, Natalie looked up at the casino's logo. Janus was the Roman god with two faces, one pointed toward the past, the other facing the future. It struck her as rather ironic, given what she was doing here, seeking out someone from her past in order to get answers so that the future could be settled.

The moment she entered the casino, the Vegas phenomena took hold. It was like stepping into a world where time did not matter or even make an appearance. There was only a sense of "now."

Because in Natalie's experience she'd discovered that bartenders knew the inner workings of any establishment they worked for better than anyone else, she made her way to the first bar she saw within the casino.

The bartender in attendance was a gregarious man in his early forties. He had a quick, sexy smile, which was probably one of the main reasons he'd been hired. His name tag identified him as Kevin.

Moving to her end of the bar, Kevin asked, "What'll it be, pretty lady?"

"Information." She saw a dubious look cross his brow. To counter that, she took out her badge. Granted she wasn't here in an official capacity, but Kevin didn't need to know that. "Were you on duty last night?"

Kevin began to wipe the gleaming black surface of the bar. "You mean during the gala?"

"Yes."

The smile gracing his lips was a satisfied one. Last night had obviously been profitable for him, she judged. "I caught an extra shift."

She took out Candace's photograph and carefully placed it on the bar. "Did you happen to see this woman there?"

The bartender glanced at the picture. Mild interest turned to recognition. "You mean Candace Rothchild? Yeah, she was here, loud and brassy as always. But not for long," he added, looking rather disappointed. There was always a circus when Candace was around, Natalie thought. "She and the boss had at it and then he had our head of security escort her out."

She latched on to the first part of his statement. "They argued? About what?"

He shook his head. "Couldn't tell you. Too far away for anything but body language," he confessed.

"And the head of security?" she asked.

"He got her to leave."

She leaned in over the bar. "Tell me about him."

"Don't know much," the bartender admitted. "Just that his name's Matt Shaffer. Boss flew him in from L.A., where he was head of security for Montgomery Enterprises."

There was no avoiding it, she thought darkly. She was going to have to talk to Matt. The thought left her cold. "Do you know where I can find him right now?"

Kevin glanced at his watch. "He should be in his office. On the second floor, toward the rear." He gave her the numbers of the rooms where the monitors that kept watch over the casino guests as they tried their luck against the house were located.

Taking out a twenty, she placed it on the bar. "Thanks for your help."

Kevin slipped the bill into his vest pocket. "Any time, lovely lady," he called after her. "Any time."

She debated going up the stairs, then decided on the elevator. The car that took her up to the second floor was empty. Natalie stepped out of the elevator, looked around to get her bearings and then walked toward the rear of the floor.

"Into the Valley of Death rode the six hundred," she silently recited, digging deep for a line from a poem by Tennyson. Wrapping her hand around a brass handle, she opened one of the glass doors and walked in.

The woman whose desk was closest to the door looked up. "You can't come in here. This is a restricted area."

Natalie already had her ID in her hand and held it up. "I'm looking for Matt Shaffer," she told the woman.

God, even saying his name made her mouth go dry. She was supposed to be over him, to have moved on with her life. What happened?

The woman began to answer her. "He's—"

"Right here."

The deep voice came from behind her. Natalie felt every single nerve ending go on tactical alert at the same moment that all the hairs at the back of her neck stood up. Eight years had passed, but she would have recognized his voice anywhere.

* * * * *

Why did Matt Shaffer leave heiress-turned-cop
Natalie Rothchild?
What does he know about the death
of Natalie's twin sister?
Come and meet these two reunited lovers and learn
the secrets of the Rothchild family in
THE HEIRESS'S 2-WEEK AFFAIR
by USA TODAY bestselling author
Marie Ferrarella.
The first book in Silhouette® Romantic Suspense's
wildly romantic new continuity,
LOVE IN 60 SECONDS!
Available April 2009.

CELEBRATE
60 YEARS
OF PURE READING PLEASURE
WITH **HARLEQUIN**®!

Look for Silhouette®
Romantic Suspense in April!

Love In 60 Seconds
Bright lights. Big city. Hearts in overdrive.

Silhouette® Romantic Suspense is celebrating
Harlequin's 60th Anniversary with six stories that
promise to bring readers the glitz of Las Vegas,
the danger of revenge, the mystery of a missing
diamond, and family scandals.

**Look for the first title, *The Heiress's 2-Week Affair*
by *USA TODAY* bestselling author
Marie Ferrarella, on sale in April!**

His 7-Day Fiancée by **Gail Barrett**	May
The 9-Month Bodyguard by **Cindy Dees**	June
Prince Charming for 1 Night by **Nina Bruhns**	July
Her 24-Hour Protector by **Loreth Anne White**	August
5 minutes to Marriage by **Carla Cassidy**	September

REQUEST YOUR FREE BOOKS!

2 FREE NOVELS PLUS 2 FREE GIFTS!

Silhouette® Desire

Passionate, Powerful, Provocative!

YES! Please send me 2 FREE Silhouette Desire® novels and my 2 FREE gifts (gifts are worth about $10). After receiving them, if I don't wish to receive any more books, I can return the shipping statement marked "cancel". If I don't cancel, I will receive 6 brand-new novels every month and be billed just $4.05 per book in the U.S. or $4.74 per book in Canada, plus 25¢ shipping and handling per book and applicable taxes, if any*. That's a savings of almost 15% off the cover price! I understand that accepting the 2 free books and gifts places me under no obligation to buy anything. I can always return a shipment and cancel at any time. Even if I never buy another book, the two free books and gifts are mine to keep forever.

225 SDN ERVX   326 SDN ERVM

Name	(PLEASE PRINT)	
Address		Apt. #
City	State/Prov.	Zip/Postal Code

Signature (if under 18, a parent or guardian must sign)

Mail to the Silhouette Reader Service:
IN U.S.A.: P.O. Box 1867, Buffalo, NY 14240-1867
IN CANADA: P.O. Box 609, Fort Erie, Ontario L2A 5X3

Not valid to current subscribers of Silhouette Desire books.

Want to try two free books from another line?
Call 1-800-873-8635 or visit www.morefreebooks.com.

* Terms and prices subject to change without notice. N.Y. residents add applicable sales tax. Canadian residents will be charged applicable provincial taxes and GST. Offer not valid in Quebec. This offer is limited to one order per household. All orders subject to approval. Credit or debit balances in a customer's account(s) may be offset by any other outstanding balance owed by or to the customer. Please allow 4 to 6 weeks for delivery. Offer available while quantities last.

Your Privacy: Silhouette Books is committed to protecting your privacy. Our Privacy Policy is available online at www.eHarlequin.com or upon request from the Reader Service. From time to time we make our lists of customers available to reputable third parties who may have a product or service of interest to you. If you would prefer we not share your name and address, please check here. ☐

SDES08R

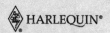
HARLEQUIN®

INTRIGUE

B.J. DANIELS

FIVE BROTHERS

ONE MARRIAGE-PACT
RACE TO THE HITCHING POST

WHITEHORSE
MONTANA
The Corbetts

SHOTGUN BRIDE

Available April 2009

Catch all five adventures in
this new exciting miniseries
from B.J. Daniels!

COMING NEXT MONTH
Available April 14, 2009

#1933 THE UNTAMED SHEIK—Tessa Radley
Man of the Month
Whisking a suspected temptress to his desert palace seems the
only way to stop her...until unexpected attraction flares and he
discovers she may not be what he thought after all.

#1934 BARGAINED INTO HER BOSS'S BED—Emilie Rose
The Hudsons of Beverly Hills
He'll do anything to get what he wants—including seduce his
assistant to keep her from quitting!

#1935 THE MORETTI SEDUCTION—Katherine Garbera
Moretti's Legacy
This charming tycoon has never heard the word *no*—until now.
Attracted to his business rival, he finds himself in a fierce battle
both in the boardroom...and the bedroom.

#1936 DAKOTA DADDY—Sara Orwig
Stetsons & CEOs
Determined to buy a ranch from his former lover and family rival,
he's shocked to discover he's a father! Now he'll stop at nothing
short of seduction to get his son.

#1937 PRETEND MISTRESS, BONA FIDE BOSS—
Yvonne Lindsay
Rogue Diamonds
His plan had been to proposition his secretary into being his
companion for the weekend. But he *didn't* plan on wanting more
than just a business relationship....

#1938 THE HEIR'S SCANDALOUS AFFAIR—
Jennifer Lewis
The Hardcastle Progeny
When the mysterious woman he spent a passionate night with
returns to tell him he may be a Hardcastle, he wonders what a
Hardcastle man should do to get her back in his bed.

SDCNMBPA0309